10/3

DEAD DRUNK

Richard Johnson

Chapter 1
No Recess

"Hope you like sitting through first grade again, motherfucker."

Charlie Campbell chugged a strong rum and coke as he changed several grades on the computer. Subbing over the summer was always a hassle, but today's shenanigans took the cake. However, with a little creative record keeping, he evened the score with one tiny terror named Markus.

The balding thirty-year-old took another swig and let out a tiny belch as his class returned from lunch. Having already dealt with fistfights, crying episodes and missing lunch money, Charlie hoped the stiff cocktail would get him through the afternoon. Still, he knew days like this tended to pick up steam.

"Class, let's get it together," he said, flicking the lights on and off as paper wads and curses whizzed about the room. They didn't even pretend to stop jacking around. In fact, they got worse, so Charlie changed tactics. "If you're quiet we can have recess at the end of—"

An eraser flew right past his head and bounced off the chalkboard, blanketing him with dust.

"Who threw that?"

No answer.

This group was a gnat's hair away from setting him off, but he couldn't complain. While it was an odd job for someone who hated kids, Charlie loved that he could skip work whenever he wanted. Depending on the hangover, whenever he wanted was about three times a week.

The sub fanned himself with a folder as he handed out worksheets and wondered why the air-conditioning wasn't working. He then retreated to his desk to sip his drink and kick his feet up. Like most inner-city classrooms, this deathtrap was chockfull of black mold, lead paint and asbestos. Oddly enough, the parking lot was filled with brand-new cars.

A little boy with a stutter approached timidly and asked to sharpen his pencil. Charlie pointed to an old electric sharpener on his desk, and a girl shouted, "We don't get to use that. Miss Marsh says we always breakin' it."

"I'll do it." Charlie sharpened the pencil, only to turn around and find several students lined up behind him. He did a few more but the line only grew longer. "This is getting ridiculous. Your pencils didn't all break at once." Charlie checked over the new arrivals. "These are fine, go sit down." He turned to the last student in line. "Markus, I sharpened that two minutes ago."

"It broke." This statement was technically correct since Markus did break the pencil seconds after the teacher sharpened it the first time.

"We're done here," Charlie said, fighting the urge to hold his young nemesis upside down over the trash can. "Use crayons if you have to, but I'm unplugging this."

"I don't have crayons," another student said.

"Borrow one then."

"Hey, he stole my crayon."

Charlie glanced at his watch and noted he only had two more hours left in that particular dump. He could handle it. Maybe.

"Teacher, I gotta make one," a small boy wearing cornrows said.

"Make what, Dantel?"

The boy held his rear. "I gotta make a doodoo."

"Me too," added a pudgy kid with a squished face.

By this time, Markus simply had to get in on the action. "I think I'm gonna squirt my pants."

A dreaded bathroom trip was going to happen whether they needed one or not because Charlie knew these kids weren't above pissing their pants to make him look bad.

"I want two single file lines." He prepared for the worst.

The students pushed their way to the door, knocking books off desks, kicking pencils across the floor and shoving each other for position.

"Sit back down, that's not how you do it." Three tries later, the class was ready. "I want complete silence. That means no talking, no touching."

They entered the hallway with a flood of general horse-play and grab-assery that let Charlie know just how badly this was about to go. He glared at Markus, who was now gyrating as if he were having a seizure. "Why are you dancing? I mean seriously?"

"I wasn't. If I was dancing, I'd be doing this."

The class roared with approval as the seven-year-old popped dance moves that would make a bar slut blush.

"Check out these moves, Mr. Campbell."

"Just knock it off and get in line." They arrived at the restrooms moments later, having broken every rule in the book. Luckily, the administrators were out golfing that day and Charlie's lack of classroom management would fly under the radar once again.

"Two in at a time. You have a minute."

The first boys went in and immediately turned the hand dryer into a beat-box. Charlie ran in to find the sinks were already clogged with paper towels and the floor soaked.

"Get out now," he said through clenched teeth.

All hell broke loose in the hallway as Charlie unclogged the sink. Blood pressure rising, he came out to find a girl pinning Markus by his throat against the wall while the other students shouted things ranging between, "Hit that punk," to "Get that bitch, Markus."

He somehow managed to separate the feral children while dodging their flailing appendages. "What happened?"

The girl's lips began to quiver. "He said my momma's head look like a vegetable."

Markus grinned. "No, I didn't. You need to stop trippin', girl." His case was hurt by the fact that he'd been caught lying approximately twelve times that day.

Charlie sighed. It was no wonder his hair had started falling out in clumps.

Another teacher burst into the hallway and gave him the stink eye. "What's going on out here? We're trying to take a test." She stared down the little girl. "Don't make me get your momma from the lunchroom."

Charlie hoped the tirade was over, but she turned her figurative guns on him next. "You need to get these kids under control. Runnin' around all crazy. That's probably why you're still a substitute."

"Go fuck yourself," Charlie said.

Actually, it's what he wanted to say instead of standing there like a whipped dog, which is what he did. Back in his days of fast living and no consequences, the words would have rolled off his tongue without a second thought. Those days were long gone.

The harpy's door slammed shut. "Damn, Mr. Campbell got told," Markus said, and the students lost it once again.

Charlie clenched his fists tightly and narrowly avoided dropping the mother lode of f-bombs. "Oh, you think it's funny Markus? Go to the office, now! The rest of you line up. Any talking, touching, dancing or singing and you're joining him."

He read them the riot act back in the classroom. "Put your heads down and keep your mouths shut. I'm not playing. No story time, no snacks and definitely no recess. You blew it."

Returning to his desk, he got his phone out and found a text message waiting from his stoner landlord.

"R u rdy to get fkd up tnite?"

Charlie Campbell's mouth twisted into a crooked smile as he pictured the upcoming bachelor party. He'd never been more ready for anything in his life.

Chapter 2
Boys' Night Out

Charlie jumped into his rusty Ford Bronco and reached under the front seat to grab a worn-out metal flask. "Hello, old friend," he said and took a healthy pull. The whiskey burned going down and he started to choke on the ninety-degree rotgut. It was this poor attention to detail that had led to Charlie's station in life.

After struggling to get the truck started, he finally sped away to the soothing rap-reggae sounds of 311 blaring out the windows. His shitty workweek had finally drawn to a close, and it was time to make his daily escape from the shadier part of town.

The truck soon approached the yard of the newly built, state of the art mega-prison. It was here that Charlie carried out a daily ritual of flipping off the inmates while honking the horn. One prisoner in particular, a stocky, dreadlocked beast of a man, always seemed to take it personally. This made Charlie smile because even though his own life sucked, at least he wasn't that guy. He hit the gas and left the stress of the day and the ominous prison behind him.

Turning his thoughts to the weekend's festivities, he realized his old fraternity buddies would already be at the apartment. Joining them would be several co-workers of Blake, the groom to be.

Blake was a consistent one-upper and bullshitter, but the fast-talking stockbroker knew how to throw a party. Unfortunately, his two sets of friends clashed, and the volatile mix of high-class and white trash was a powder keg ready for a spark.

Charlie jammed his truck into the narrow parking space behind his apartment and jogged up to the old stone three-flat. He lived on the second floor with his roommate Trent, while Smokey, their friend and owner of the building, lived up top in an art studio.

Years earlier, Smokey had water-bonged his way out of college and ended up in his parents' basement. With nothing but time on his hands and a healthy imagination, he somehow developed a knack for making art out of junk. One morning after a mean acid trip, Smokey discovered he'd welded a masterpiece out of a muffler, the neighbor's mailbox and an old Schwinn bicycle. The sculpture tastefully depicted a naked George Bush riding backwards on a striped Zebra-corn. Art critics compared it to a Don Quixote-like vision where the ex-president tilted at non-existent weapons of mass destruction. It was his big break.

Sean Penn purchased the "art" for several hundred grand and Smokey took the cash and never looked back. He used the windfall to buy the old building and set up a studio for himself. However, the easy living stifled his art, and he couldn't even get off the couch, much less fire up the welder. Cartoons, a never-ending supply of cereal and a massive stash of pot didn't help.

Still, he did manage to make the apartment eco-friendly with some renovations and was now bringing in steady rent checks.

At the moment, the long-haired burnout focused on finishing off an expertly-rolled joint on his front porch. He didn't even notice the police cruiser roll up. A portly officer came towards him and pointed angrily.

"Is that a joint I see, scumbag?"

"Sherlock Holmes, I presume?" Smokey blew a stream of smoke into the officer's face and then winked at Charlie as he came up the stairs.

"Well?" The cop took off his dark aviator glasses with a flourish, and it was obvious he had practiced the maneuver quite often.

Smokey took another drag. "You tell me."

"It is a joint, and it's my last one, asshole," the cop said.

Smokey made a half-baked apology to the man, who happened to be Charlie's roommate, Trent. "My bad. I thought there was some left in the medicine cabinet."

Trent glared at his friend. "There was. That's the one you're smoking right now, douche."

"Oh yeah."

"And this is why you're the worst fucking landlord in the city," Trent said.

"And you're the worst cop in the city."

"Point taken. But you can get back in my good graces by scoring some blow. These strippers aren't gonna bang us for our good looks." He pointed to Charlie. "This guy knows what I'm talking about."

"Fine. I'll call Julio. Man you're a pain in the ass."

"Remember, no laced shit or I'll nab your buddy for walking while Puerto Rican. Last time I thought clowns were chasing me, and you know I hate clowns." Trent jumped back in the cruiser. "Anyways, text and let me know where to go. I've got two *dancers* on call, so make sure people save some cash."

The police radio crackled.

"I gotta jet. Don't forget to buy that shit." He flipped on his lights and pulled away, wondering why his friend was such a mooch.

"Fuckin' pig," Smokey said while turning to Charlie. "Like I didn't know it was his last joint."

Charlie laughed. "I figured. Who's here?"

"Blake and some of his friends. Plus Jim."

"His wife let him come after all?"

"Yep. Other than that, Gay Mike and Left-Nut made it. Oh, and Big Rob's here. He took a massive dump and clogged your toilet, by the way."

Charlie groaned. "God damn it. This isn't the first time he's done that."

"And it reeks like a dead skunk." Smokey flicked his roach into the garden below, forgetting he would have to pick it up later.

Big Rob greeted them at the door and then turned back inside. "Charlie's here, so stop wiping your asses on his pillow." The bearded, six foot six mixed-martial artist donned a beer helmet packing Jack Daniels on one side and Coke on the other. He pulled a straw from his mouth with a hand the size of a catcher's mitt before asking, "Want a pull, muchacho?"

"I'm gonna get changed first," Charlie said.

He got several high-fives on his way past the living room bar and noted that drinking games were already in full swing. The host got dressed and finally joined the party.

A skinny white-haired rogue approached and handed Charlie a can of ice-cold beer. "Long time no see."

"Hey, Left-Nut, how's it hangin'?"

"Like usual, massive and right down the middle."

His name was Matt Tucker but nobody had called him that in years. The story was that Matt had been riding a bike during a thunderstorm when a lightning strike made him crap his pants, turned his hair white and caused one of his testicles to burst. And so Left-Nut was born.

As Charlie cracked open his beer, another friend known affectionately as Gay Mike walked over from the kitchen, grinning from ear to ear. "Hey, sexy, it's about time you showed up. I've been waiting to do some body shots."

Gay Mike set down a blue bottle of Reposada and two shot glasses on the table. The veterinarian wasn't gay by any means, but did have an odd habit of making comments with homosexual undertones. Like Left-Nut, the nickname had stuck.

"It's a little early for tequila... ah, what the hell. I think I'll have mine in the glass, though. How are the animals treating you?" Charlie asked.

"I can't complain. I'm making good money and my hours are cake." Gay Mike leaned in. "How are the animals treating *you?*"

Charlie chuckled. "Not good. I think my blood pressure's skyrocketing. It's like they always know exactly how to piss me off and then do it."

"You should seriously find something else to do. I could hire you as a vet tech."

"Yeah, sure," Charlie said as his eyes glazed over.

"Anyways, back to me. We got a new assistant last week who is a total smoke-show. She knows it, too," Mike said. "I think she's caught me staring at her tits like five times already."

"Shit, maybe I should work for you."

"She reminds me of that chick you nailed in college. I can't remember the name, you know the softball player with the—"

"Carrie Evans," Charlie said wistfully, remembering better days.

"That chick was hot. She was in my psych class, and I couldn't concentrate because I had a boner the whole time. Those were the days, man. You could fall out of a boat and land in pussy back then."

Charlie nodded. "Now I'd be lucky to hit water."

There was some yelling from the bathroom. "Who clogged the shitter? It looks like someone tried to flush a dead rabbit."

"Damn, I forgot." Charlie slammed the shot and headed for the kitchen cabinet. He returned a minute later with purple rubber gloves and a plunger, ready to battle the unholy beast.

Big Rob was currently shirtless in the living room and rapping to an old Tupac song. His arms were still massive, but his gut was now equally impressive. He paused his performance. "Be careful in there, last night was two for one Whoppers at Burger King."

Charlie emerged moments later, gasping for air. "Jesus, it's like you gave birth to Rosemary's baby in there."

"I'll go in the yard next time if you want."

Charlie pictured the old lady on the first floor having a coronary. "Just use a courtesy flush for God's sake. The bathroom smells like a damned nursing home. You need to start eating more fiber or something. It's like you literally crapped an entire ham. Intact."

"I'm on the no carb diet." He patted his substantial belly. "Nothing but meat."

The sight of another friend coming from the kitchen with a cigar in one hand and a glass of wine in the other caught Charlie's attention. "Right when I thought Mike was the queerest guy I knew, you show up drinking wine at a bachelor party."

Jim, Charlie's best friend from childhood, pulled up a seat. "Gay? I'm not the one wearing purple gloves, faggot."

Charlie nodded. "Touché. Still... wine? Are you getting all sophisticated on us?"

"What? I like wine. I always have and—"

"Oh come on, your wife wants you to drive home tonight, doesn't she?" Charlie knew something was up. Jim was ready for a church potluck and everyone else was liable to piss on the couch.

"Cindy knows how we act when we get together. She might be a bitch, but she's not stupid."

Of course his wife was right. The average intelligence of the group dropped five points every time another one entered the room, and would go down five more every hour they spent together. By the end of the night there would be a bunch of slack-jawed idiots trying to hump or fight anything not nailed to the ground.

Rob jumped in. "She'll have big dongs waving in her face tonight so you might as well cut loose too." It was sound advice, even if it did come from a sweaty and shirtless ogre sporting a beer helmet.

Jen, Blake's gorgeous fiancée, was having her party across town, and most of the group's significant others would be attending. The girls were actually going to see a transvestite fashion show and finish the night off at a dance club — tame compared to what their men had in mind.

The bachelor noticed the discussion and saw the glass of wine. "This ain't a book club. Get this pussy a shot of Wild Turkey." Blake made gobbling noises and flapped his arms.

Peer pressure could be a bitch even for thirty-year-olds, and Jim saw the looks he was getting from his friends.

"Fine, but someone's taking my car keys and I don't wanna know who."

Charlie had a huge smile on his face as he went for the Wild Turkey in the freezer. The shenanigans had begun.

Chapter 3
A Pale Horse

The noise and blood-alcohol levels in the apartment steadily rose as the afternoon wore on. Porn played on the big screen while music blared, and the drinking games got out of hand. Conversations focused on sports and loose women while the lies about salaries and sex floated around as thick as the pot smoke filling the room.

Meanwhile, Charlie was striking out in a card game called "asshole" and had started to get suspicious. "All right, which one of you shit-heels is cheating?" he said while dealing the cards. Left-Nut, Jim and Big Rob stayed cool, so Charlie focused on his friend named Vidu. "You look guilty and your last hand was too good. Take five drinks."

The "asshole" assigned drinks only while dealing, but anyone else could return the favor afterwards, and this often led to swift payback.

Vidu, a short and wiry Sri Lankan native, chugged his beer. "What can I say? I'm lucky with cards and women. It's a gift from the gods."

He'd been in the States for ten years but still had a thick accent and a horrible grasp of American culture. Why the gang put up with him was anyone's guess.

"Luck better find you a wife soon or you'll be back to humping monkeys in the jungle," Charlie said with a wink.

"Don't worry, ladies love the Vidu." This was quite an overstatement, and with a two-month deadline to get a green card, things looked bleak indeed.

Blake knocked the cards out of Charlie's hands. "Our limo is gonna be here in twenty minutes so start getting ready." He leaned in with an arched eyebrow. "By the way, Vidu's been cheating the whole time."

Everyone threw their cards down and Charlie wiped his brow in relief. His buzz was growing, and it was way too early for that. He looked to Vidu. "Luck, huh? You just earned yourself a prairie fire shot at the bar."

"You make your own luck," Vidu replied.

Blake called everyone in for the game plan. "Gentlemen, the first stop's a little Irish pub by the name of Drunken McPunchee's." The cheers he expected never materialized.

Smokey in particular wasn't having it. "That place is all Lincoln Park trust-fund babies. We should go across the street to Ned and Eileen's. They've got cheap drinks, no lines and no one-percenters."

Blake stifled the dissent quickly. "First off, smelly hippy, someone has to pay taxes so you druggies can get free needles and hepatitis medicine. More importantly, Ned and Eileen's is a fucking dive, and the only bush we'll see there is the old hag that owns the place. McPunchee's has dance music and co-eds, and tonight's Mailbox Night. Single, drunk chicks. There's a slim chance that even Vidu could get laid."

"Who's getting married again?" Mike asked.

"I'm not married yet, gay-wad," Blake shot back. "Look, if you want to see a drag-queen show, meet up with the bachelorette party. If you're coming with us, grow a pair."

"Real funny," Mike said. "Maybe I will go and see your fiancée tonight."

Moments later they assembled outside. The sun had set but it was still brutally hot, and the Midwest humidity clung to them like a needy ex-girlfriend. It had been a long summer for everyone.

"Where's the damn limo?" Left-Nut said and raised an ice-cold bottle to his forehead.

Smokey had a smug look on his face. "Global warming's a bitch, isn't it?"

Charlie had heard this spiel for the last time. "Oh please. You put up some solar panels and suddenly you're greener than Al Gore's cock? Spare me. Nobody is buying it dude."

"There's nothing wrong with going granola," Smokey replied. "Have to balance out the republi-nazis, and you know the crunchy chicks love it."

"Ooh, look at me, I'm Captain Planet because I wipe my ass with newspapers and take hobo baths," Charlie said.

"Laugh it up, fuckers. But hasn't it been super hot lately around here?"

"It is summer," one of Blake's nameless co-workers said and loosened his tie.

Smokey was unbothered by his total lack of support. "When we dry up like China did and shit hits the fan, you'll come knocking. This place is totally off the grid, baby. I've got solar power, charcoal water filters, the whole nine yards. I've been getting pointers from that *Doomsday Preppers* show."

"Screw China. After invading Taiwan they can all starve to death as far as I'm concerned," Jim said. "Plus, the savages eat dogs."

Blake threw his hands up. "Come on, no politics at my bachelor party. Talk about socket wrenches or pussy or something. Hell, talk about socket wrenches *and* pussy."

Big Rob pointed skyward. "That sure looks like something to talk about."

"Holy shit," Left-Nut said as the bottle slipped from his hand and shattered on the road.

Beyond belief, clearly appearing on the rising full moon was the image of a horse, outlined in green and standing on its hind legs. A pale horse.

"It looks like the Fourth Horseman of the Apocalypse," Jim stated breathlessly. No one challenged the ex-altar boy, and the drunken group stood in stunned silence for a few long seconds.

Finally, Charlie spoke up. "Do any of you morons watch the news?" Blank stares. "Seriously, nobody even heard about this the past month?"

Left-Nut shook his head. "Spit it out already."

"You can stop clutching your pearls because that's an advertisement for Pale Horse Beer."

There were some sighs of relief and a few lies about knowing the whole time, but Big Rob still stared up in confusion. "Do you mean astronauts are up on the moon right now?"

Charlie bit his tongue. Rob had never been all that bright, and after countless blows to the head was even less so. "Nobody's up there. The company's using some high powered lasers beamed up from northern Canada."

"Oh, cool," Rob said.

"They had to keep airplanes out of the sky for miles around so they wouldn't get burned up on accident."

"Sounds expensive," Gay Mike said.

"Like a million dollars a minute," Charlie said. "Still, a ton of people are gonna see it. But you'd have to be a complete moron to fall for marketing like that." The eerie design blinked a few times and then disappeared. "Looks like the show's over."

The limo finally pulled up, and everyone piled into the pimped-out ride and went right back to drinking. ESPN played on flat screens while rap music and a disco ball set the tone as the hectic pace of the party picked up once more.

Blake set down two paper sacks. "Okay, we're gonna do boat races so none of you dildos sober up." Inside were two lukewarm bottles of strawberry Mad Dog 20-20, breakfast of winos all over the world. "It's my college friends versus my work friends. You guys always talk smack so now we'll see who can back it up."

After some mild grumbling, the two teams squared off. The game was a simple one. A player would chug and then pass the bottle down the line, and the anchor had to finish it off. The first team to finish would earn coveted shit-talking rights for the rest of the night.

The race began, and even with Vidu's lackluster performance, the college friends dominated. Of course, having Big Rob made the difference. After all, the man was legendary in the sporting world for guzzling a bottle of whiskey on the way into the ring before demolishing an opponent.

Left-Nut was quick to stir the pot. "I haven't seen anyone lose that bad since the Jamaican bobsled team. You boys ever drank before?"

Blake's overdressed friend named Cliff fought back. "First off, you guys had Andre the Giant over there. The guy's head is like a watermelon," he said and gestured to Rob who was tucking into a cheeseburger pulled from one of his pockets. "Second off, who gives a shit? You can drink a lot, big deal. Put it on a resume and see if it gets you a job."

It was too early for the griping to start, so the bachelor stepped in to moderate. "Listen up, ladies. We're gonna be at McPunchee's in a minute. The limo's coming back at ten for the next stop, so if you wander off, tough shit."

Charlie raised his hand. "Where are we going at ten?"

"Patience, young Padawan," Blake said with an impish grin, enjoying his control over the itinerary. "It's another of my favorite stomping grounds. I promise it'll be fun."

Upon arriving, the gang clambered once more into the sweltering heat and humidity that was thick enough to suck the breath right out of a person's lungs. Luckily, the line was short.

McPunchee's was a dive that specialized in watered down drinks and cheesy gimmicks. Mailbox Night was one such gimmick where drinkers had the chance to meet complete strangers by wearing address labels. If a person wanted to flirt, they simply dropped a note in the corresponding mailbox. It was dumb, but the place was packed.

They grabbed their tags and spread out to eye the female talent while Charlie went to buy a round of beer. A perky brunette sporting a ridiculously short skirt came over as a Guns-n-Roses song came on the jukebox. She had a skanky emo look going and he definitely approved.

"I need to open a tab."

She leaned forward, flashing the balding man a fake smile and scrunching her cleavage together while grabbing

Charlie's almost maxed out credit card. "Sure thing. What can I get you?"

He smiled back. "Fifteen Pale Horses."

Chapter 4
Love Letters

Charlie chatted with his closest pals while the others shot pool or hit on women. The crew saw each other less often now, so it was good to hear old stories of bar fights, hazing pledges, cheating on tests and catching each other masturbating in the quad.

But reality had proven to be quite different from their time at the dilapidated fraternity house. Where school had been one big party, adult life was one giant hangover. Crappy jobs, failed relationships, crushed dreams or the drudgery of suburban life had taken a toll on all of them.

The trip down memory lane conjured up better times, but also reminded them of all that had changed. Panama City spring breaks became antiquing in Door County. Late nights partying turned into late nights meeting deadlines. A whirlwind of morally challenged women morphed into a nagging wife, or even worse, the dim glow of internet porn in a lonely bedroom. In a nutshell, adulthood sucked.

Jim cleared his throat. "I wanted to let you guys know that Cindy's pregnant. Obviously, this is a big deal for us."

Charlie slapped him on the back and leaned in. "Who's the dad?" Everyone busted up. "No, but that's awesome news. Congrats."

"She's due around Thanksgiving, and we're gonna wait to find out the sex."

"I'm sure you don't have enough testosterone to pump out anything with a dick, so I'm guessing it's a girl," Left-Nut said dryly and wandered to the dance floor to harass several women minding their own business.

Jim flashed the white-haired jerk a dirty look. "Says the guy with one testicle."

"Don't mind the sour grapes," Blake said loudly and then summoned a round of Jager Bombs in celebration.

Charlie wondered what was wrong with the rest of them, himself included. Vidu could barely speak English and was on the verge of deportation. Big Rob had gained seventy pounds and hadn't fought in two years. Gay Mike was un-dateable, and Smokey was down to his last brain cells. Finally, there was the walking hard-on known as Left-Nut. Charlie watched him get shot down by four girls in thirty seconds and keep right on trucking. Getting laid was a numbers game, he always said.

Vidu stumbled off to the bathroom and Charlie saw his chance to get even. Having blown most of his money on the round of beers, he settled on something more devious than buying a disgusting shot, and it wouldn't cost a dime.

He grabbed two blank letters from the mailbox station and addressed the first to a stacked college girl that he'd noticed earlier sucking down dry martinis like water. The schoolteacher marked it, "Urgent: Special Delivery," and the words flew feverishly from his pen.

I could not help but notice how gorgeous and sexually active you are looking in the glow of the neon Budweiser sign. Would you like some alcohol beverage? Maybe a fruited drink like on Sex and the City? I would like very much to make love to your large American breasts. Are you wealthy? Please write back to mailbox #102 or see me at the table next to the dartboard. I am wearing an orange Ed Hardy shirt.

Dearly yours,
Vidu

P.S. Do you have any diseases?
P.P.S. If you are a lesbian or a bitch please give this letter to your short friend that is dressed like a hooker.

Charlie addressed the second letter to Vidu.

Hi there, stranger.
I saw you the moment I walked in and just had to drop
you a few lines. You're really cute. Make sure you come see
me tonight! I'm kinda shy but would love a big hug.
XOXO,
#70

Charlie dropped the letters into the numbered slots and casually went back to his seat to find Left-Nut complaining about stuck-up women while Big Rob wolfed down expired pickled eggs.

Remembering the gross bathroom incident from earlier, Charlie pushed the jar away and took on the lecturing tone he often used when speaking to his giant friend. "Stop eating all this junk if you're staying at my place. The pipes can't handle it."

"Fine, I promise I won't use your toilet."

"That's not what I mean. What I'm really getting at is, if you're ever going to fight again you need to lose weight. Honestly, you're starting to look like a sumo wrestler."

Now it was Rob's turn to get annoyed. "You want to act like my trainer again? You did such a great job the last time," he said, his voice dripping with sarcasm. It hadn't worked out so hot, and he still blamed Charlie for his stalled career.

"I just want you to take care of yourself. You keep living like this and you won't be around long."

Rob looked down. "I guess I could stand to lose a couple of pounds." He always ended up agreeing with Charlie.

"You know I need to get in shape too. How about I start running with you next week?"

Rob's face brightened. "It could be like old times again, except this time I won't get—"

"Check out the buns on her," Left-Nut said and pointed at an attractive girl swaying on the dance floor to a crappy indie-rock song, the same girl that Charlie had just written to. "She's giving me a five-dollar footlong." Vidu agreed and the trap was set.

Twenty minutes later the girl went to the mailbox and discovered the letter. A sour look crossed her face and she scanned the bar for the creeper in the day-glow shirt.

In the meantime, Blake gathered the party together for yet another drinking game. "Okay, guys, it's time for credit card roulette. Put your card into this lovely hat, and if I pull your card, you buy a round. The only catch is the buyer picks the shot. We'll pull two. Any questions?" There weren't. "Good. Pony up." He handed a trucker hat sporting giant boobs to Cliff.

Charlie tossed his card in, knowing it couldn't cover one shot much less a round. For him, it really was roulette. Cliff gathered the other cards and then stared upwards at Rob. "I need one from the big guy."

"Like anyone would give me credit. Dude, I've got like two pairs of underwear to my name."

Cliff looked at Rob with a hint of disgust. "Someone needs to cover for cheap-ass here and add another card." Jim stepped up since he'd been paying for the loveable loser's tab all night anyway.

Blake pulled out the first card. "Jim Evans." He shuffled the cards in the hat and then pulled out one more. "What are the odds? Jim again, sucks to be you."

"What the hell?"

"That's the breaks," Blake said. "Cindy is gonna flip out when she checks your bank statement."

"She probably will." Now resigned to dropping a bunch of cash, Jim wanted to have some fun with it. "Since it's loser's choice, you're gonna have a cement mixer and a dead Nazi. Suck on that."

Mike groaned. "God, I hate these stupid games."

"Rules are rules," Cliff said. "I'm surprised Jim picked those shots since he has to drink them too."

Jim's smile evaporated. "Scratch that order. Two rounds of cherry pucker it is."

Cliff smiled. "What was that about prom night earlier?"

"Whatever, asshole. Let's do this." Jim flagged a cute waitress and they downed the fruity shots and went back to their conversations.

Charlie put his plan into action since Vidu was looking thoroughly sauced. "Let's see if we have any mail." They didn't, and with Left-Nut's lines like, "You're ugly, but you intrigue me," it was no surprise.

But Vidu had apparently hit pay dirt, and his eyes lit up as he read the note. "I need to find this number seventy. She needs a hot Vidu injection, stat."

They eagerly looked for Vidu's pen pal and Blake spotted the beauty first. "Bullshit. No way she wants his lame ass."

Of course, Vidu took offense to Blake's statement and responded in kind. "Don't be jealous. You're engaged, why care if I can pull more ass than you?" It was rare the awkward foreigner got a chance to lord over his arrogant friend, but now he'd have to put up or shut up.

"Seal the deal, Casanova," Blake said with a chuckle. He knew this wouldn't end well and had always enjoyed his friend's legendary meltdowns.

Normally Vidu would be petrified to approach any woman, much less a knockout like this, but tonight he'd been guzzling liquid courage in a can. He combed his greasy hair with his fingers and tucked in his shirt. "This is how it's done, boys."

"Twenty bucks says he blows it," Blake said and waved a crisp bill. No takers.

"Hey, sexy mama," Vidu said as he grabbed the alluring girl from behind and gave her a bear hug.

The vixen turned around and recoiled in disgust when she saw who held her ever so gently. "Get off me, you perverted fuckwad," she said and followed with an open palmed bitch-slap to the Sri Lankan's shocked face. As if that weren't enough, Charlie's phone was recording every glorious second, ensuring this payback would last forever.

Vidu clutched his jaw and asked with a whimper, "What was that for?"

The enraged girl ignored his question as she balled her fists and prepared to press the attack. But right before she thrashed him again, a tank-top-wearing bouncer stepped in and saved Vidu from further humiliation.

"All right, jackass, time to go." He put one meaty hand on Vidu's puny shoulder and pointed to the door.

Fearing deportation even more than another righteous ass whipping, Vidu ran out like quicksilver. "The rest of you need to go, too. We don't cater to creeps here," the meathead added, itching for an excuse to show off for the pretty girl.

Everyone was too busy gasping for air to notice how much of a prick the bouncer was, and they left without further incident. Charlie put his phone away and climbed into the waiting limo, still smiling about his dirty deed.

Chapter 5
Rock the Mic

The limo reeked of stale whiskey farts and fried food as it headed for the next stop. But the driver was forced to slam the brakes when a large number of bike riders streamed out from a side street. The biking group known as the "Happy Saturday Brigade" often snarled traffic and pissed off motorists.

Blake rolled down his window. "Out of the way, losers!"

A few riders casually flipped him off but most simply told him to have a happy Saturday.

"Society's tampons," Cliff said while staring at the motley crowd. It was an odd group, highlighted by buzz-cut lesbians in fishnets and leather-clad gimps cruising by on custom-built Big Wheels, sparklers blazing. Even stranger, Santa Clause passed by on a monstrous ten-foot tall bike.

"That's not something you see every day," Jim said as a few more freaks pedaled past.

"Never been to Gay Mike's neighborhood?" Left-Nut said and Mike answered with a healthy punch to the arm.

Blake opened an imported beer and walked towards the front of the limo. "Jugdish, step on it."

"What do you want me to do?" the driver said with an accent even thicker than Vidu's.

"Inch forward. They'll move."

The driver relented and slowly took his foot off the brakes. He got a third of the way through the mess before an onslaught of angry cyclists made him stop.

Smokey started up a chant and everyone joined in. "Go! Go! Go!"

The limo surged forward and narrowly avoided several riders, but the back end had almost cleared the crosswalk and soon enough they'd be on to the next bar.

That's when an ice-cold Big Gulp soared through an open window and blasted Vidu square in the face, drenching him completely. He did not take it well.

"I kill you, motherfucker! I kill you!" Vidu clawed at the child-locked door. "How I open this fucking shit?" Out-smarted by the door, the Sri Lankan tried to dive out the window in order to throttle the anonymous drink launcher. Luckily, the driver saw an opening, slammed on the gas, and saved Vidu from his second beat down of the evening.

After ridiculing their hapless friend for a bit, the party moved on to guessing their next destination. Wild rumors began to circulate. Cliff hoped for "General Zhou's tug-jobs" at an Asian massage parlor while Smokey believed they were en-route to a secretive, non-licensed bar that moved locations every month to avoid paying taxes.

The speculation ended abruptly when the limo stopped in front of The Study, an ordinary college bar frequented by DePaul co-eds. Left-Nut was underwhelmed. "Oh come on, we're gonna be ten years older than everyone here." His white hair didn't help with the college girls, and his lack of common decency was an even bigger turnoff.

"Tough shit," Blake said. "We leave in two hours for the last stop so get after it."

The Study resembled a library, complete with book-lined shelves, card catalogues and naughty librarians serving drinks and spankings. It was jam packed with hipsters but Cliff had already arranged for tables in the VIP section.

Charlie glanced at the books by their table and noticed everything from *War and Peace* to *You Might be a Red-neck*. However, it was a pink hardback titled *The Fine Art of Giving Blowjobs* that stood out from the rest. He flipped it open to the front. "What do you know? Gay Mike checked this out twice."

"You guys really need to stop busting my balls," Mike said defensively.

"See, he can't stop talking about male genitalia," Jim said. "It's like he's cock-crazy."

A stacked server in a sexy faux-geek outfit approached and momentarily put an end to the bash-fest. "I'm Lola and I'll be your librarian tonight. For specials we have eight dollar pitchers of Pale Horse, twelve dollar fishbowl kamikazes and half off wings." She adjusted her glasses and tapped a notebook with impeccably manicured nails. "You boys look like you're gonna be fun tonight," she added while batting long lashes.

Charlie looked away and scanned the bar. He was buzzing hard and wanted to talk to real women for once, women that didn't make their living by fleecing gullible morons.

"Oh I'm fun. You can see when you get off work," the gullible moron named Vidu said with an off-putting stare.

"You're bad. I might have to discipline you," Lola said while twirling a ruler and wondering why Vidu was soaking wet and had a large handprint on his face.

Of course, Vidu would later claim she wanted to, "Tie him up and fuck his balls out," whatever that meant.

Oblivious to the girl's charms and massive rack, Big Rob focused on other priorities. "Cheap wings sound good," he said and licked his chops.

Jim looked at his bulky friend with annoyance. "Why do you care if they're half off? Your broke-ass ran out of money an hour ago." Rob flashed the same jovial smile he always did and Jim caved as he always did. "I guess I'll take twenty—" Big Rob cleared his throat loudly in protest, and Jim sighed. "Make that fifty mild wings and a pitcher of Pale Horse." Rob nodded his approval.

Smokey's phone boomed the theme song to the show *Cops*. "I bet Trent's calling about the hookers, I mean strippers, for tonight."

"You guys really are bad," the waitress said and laughed nervously. Smokey rose from his seat with a flushed face and took the call outside while everyone finished ordering.

Charlie noticed plenty of women nearby but it didn't matter much. He had gone from being a young stud to a middle-aged loser quite some time ago, and his confidence was beyond shot.

A lanky, red-haired friend of Blake's named Bruce slammed a stack of *National Geographics* down on the table. "Next game is called Jungle Titties. Last person to find a pair buys a round of shots."

Charlie spotted a cover featuring Masai lion hunters and knew it was money in the bank. "I'm in," he said and tossed his useless credit card into the hat. Sure enough, he found some nude villagers in under a minute.

Cliff had less luck. "This game's fucking dumb," he said after losing handily.

"Pony up, and make it whiskey," Blake said.

Cliff complied and soon returned with a clinking tray of shots. However, some of the group balked at downing the harsh stuff and Big Rob graciously volunteered to put them away. He was hitting full throttle four shots later.

Someone began singing badly, and it became clear why Blake insisted on this bar. Charlie sighed. "You couldn't find something better to do than karaoke?"

"The blowjob factory was booked," Blake said with a chuckle. The truth was he worked for a South Korean firm and spent countless hours sucking up to his boss in karaoke joints. It didn't translate to being good at it, though.

Annoyed, Charlie went back to searching the bar and spotted a cute woman a few tables over. He made eye contact and surprisingly, she gave a shy smile back. So Charlie steeled his nerves and rose to make a move. This was a big step for him.

"Oh shit, I forgot to tell you something," Jim said and dragged Charlie back into his seat. "You're gonna want to hear this."

"What?" Charlie was clearly annoyed.

"My parents called and said Craig Baxter got busted for trying to suck off an undercover cop for some crack."

"Serves him right, that guy was the biggest asshole in high school," Charlie said as two guys with popped collars and heavily-gelled hair approached the comely woman.

"Yeah, he was a tool. Guy had everything handed to him and look where he is now. Karma's a bitch."

"Total silver spoon." Charlie said, barely listening as he spied on the situation a few tables over. Sure enough, the pretty-boys flagged a librarian down for shots. Game over.

"It's even worse than when he was bench pressing at soccer practice and shit his pants. Remember that?"

Charlie turned back to his friend, resigned at blowing another chance. "No, that was Left-Nut. I was the one spotting him."

At that point an emcee spoke into his microphone. "Set down those books and put your hands together for our next singer, Blake! He's hung like Bigfoot and celebrating his bachelor party tonight, so single ladies take note. This is your last chance to sample this prime beefcake."

"You paid that guy twenty bucks, didn't you?" Charlie asked and chuckled.

"Sure as hell did," Blake said with a wink as he stood up and raised his fists in glory. "Watch the panties fly," he added while sauntering towards the stage like an 80's rock star.

The pompous investor grabbed the mic as the music kicked in. *Da da da, da da da da, da da da, da da da da.* Blake nodded to the beat for a moment and then jumped into the song full tilt, giving one of the worst renditions of "Ice Ice Baby" ever known to man. His improvised dance moves were even worse.

"He looks like Frankenstein with cerebral palsy and a broom up his ass," Smokey said, stoned out of his mind. Even Blake's brown-nosing work friends couldn't take it, and several catcalls came in from the audience.

Blake finished the song a few painful minutes later and came back with his head held high and a huge smile plastered on his face. "Nailed it."

"Actually, that was shit," Left-Nut said. "And for the record, no panties reached the stage."

"Oh, come on. I saw a lot of people cheering out there."

"Those were boos."

Blake ignored reality and ordered his lackey Cliff to buy yet another round of shots. Big Rob took charge of the surplus once again.

Meanwhile, Charlie was broke and hadn't even talked to a female yet. Guessing the last stop would be a strip club, the night appeared to be a failure. "I might as well go on auto-pilot and see what happens," he said and snagged the last shot before Rob could pour it down his cavern of a mouth.

Left-Nut raised his beer in a toast. "That's the spirit. You can go pig-fishing with me."

Charlie wasn't about to start looking for fat chicks, so he settled back in with Jim and started mooching beer. As though he were experiencing drunken time travel, the night seemed to speed up and soon it was time for the next bar.

When Charlie stood, someone began to sing an Elvis song in a way that he could only describe as perfect. The voice that rang out over the speakers was as thick and velvety as the King of Rock himself. Charlie turned to see who was putting on such a solid performance.

The homeless-looking man swaying with the melody was dressed in tattered jean shorts and sported a long, brown beard. It was Big Rob.

"What the shit?" Vidu said.

The three-hundred pound fighter finished the song to raucous cheers. Then he bowed low for a standing ovation and promptly fell face first off the stage onto a table, smashing it in half and sending drinks flying. It was time to leave.

Chapter 6
The Sugar Shack

"Brains... brains!"

Big Rob cracked open his eyes to see a scrotum dangling dangerously close to his forehead. He was conscious just long enough to shove Blake halfway across the limo. This set up a chain reaction where Blake fell into Smokey's lit cigarette while crashing to the floor, tipping over two full beer cans on the way.

The driver pounded on the steering wheel. "You're going to clean that up."

Not one of the drunks paid any attention, and Blake rubbed the burn on his arm while pulling his pants up. "How many shots did Rob have anyways?"

"I lost track after ten," Jim said. "And that's on top of the two pitchers that I bought, and the beer he was stealing when people weren't paying attention."

"I thought my beer was going down smooth," Charlie said. Big Rob had learned to fish for drinks on a trip to Panama City years ago and apparently still had the skill.

"He's too drunk to go in," Bruce said while eying the sleeping giant.

"Are you gonna stop him?" Charlie replied. Rob was shit-faced, but after seeing him flick Blake across the limo like a stale booger, it was clear he was still dangerous.

Left-Nut grew impatient. "All I know is I need to see some tits and I need to see 'em now."

"I swear you're just a dick with legs," Mike said.

Jim smiled. "Sounds like Gay Mike's talking about dicks once again."

They finally arrived at their last destination, a seedy strip club called The Sugar Shack. The driver had reached the end of his patience. "Get the hell out!"

They had no choice but to bring Rob in, so they woke him up and left the trashed vehicle amidst the sound of half-empty beer bottles clanking onto the pavement. The driver flipped them off and peeled away into the night. Now they'd have to cab it home later, but their thoughts were elsewhere as they lurched towards the sleaziest spot in Chi-town.

Charlie helped his unsteady friend across the parking lot. "When we get in, sit down, drink some water and shut up."

The club itself featured a cheesy laser show, black lights and a sleazy deejay screaming while stark-naked women sold lap dances. It was a place where you could get anything for the right price, which, according to Left-Nut, was around fifty dollars. "Now this is what I'm talking about," he said while finally entering his element.

Cliff and Bruce flashed their money around by ordering thirty-dollar shots of tequila and a bottle of Dom for the bachelor. Cash was king, and within minutes, they were swarmed by a handful of teenage strippers.

With a skinny eighteen year old on his lap, Cliff decided it was time to put the peasants in their place. He looked at Vidu with a sneer. "So, Osama, how's the jihad going?"

Vidu's eyes glazed over. "Fuck your mother, you little son of a..."

Charlie put himself between them. "Why are you being such a dickhole? We're just trying to have fun." Vidu was a turd, but he was their turd.

Cliff scoffed. "I don't need a lecture from a substitute teacher. I make more money by March than you make all year. You're as pathetic as these other losers."

"Guys, not now," Blake said.

But Charlie had already lost it. "Okay fatty, how about I take you outside and stomp a mud hole in your ass?" It took a lot to push his buttons, but he could throw down if he had to.

"I've got better things to do," Cliff retorted and smacked the stripper's bottom. "You up for a dance, little girl?" The high school dropout was, and she led the jerk away to skillfully dry-hump hundreds of dollars out of him in record time.

"Don't sweat it, he made some bad trades and lost a ton of money this week," Blake said.

"No. He's an ass, but he's got a point." Charlie sighed. "What the hell happened to me?"

"You've had some bad luck," Jim said. "I bet a change of scenery would help."

"I haven't been on a date in three years and I'm stuck in a job a moron could do. Plus, I'm not getting any younger."

Mike grabbed his friend's shoulder. "You're only in your thirties bro."

"Yeah, and I've already got the bald horseshoe thing going on."

Blake had heard enough. "Fuck this pity party. You need to get your confidence back. Stop sitting around waiting for good things to happen to you and stop being such a pussy." He cracked his knuckles. "Luckily, I'm just the guy to help. I'll be right back."

Blake returned with company. "Svetlana, this is my friend, Professor Campbell. He teaches English at DePaul University." Truth was always the first casualty when it came to getting laid.

"Umm, hello." Charlie stared at his feet.

"*Milo mi* (nice to meet you)," the gorgeous brunette waitress answered back in Polish while Blake stood behind her, making a gesture in sign language for large breasts. "I'm wanting to be writer. This man said you could teach?" She batted her eyes and looked vulnerable and endearing at the same time. Charlie almost felt guilty.

"Ahh, yeah. Sure I'd be willing to um, to see what kind of writing style you have and give you some pointers." Charlie did his best impression of a haughty professor.

"*Dobry* (good). I get off in hour. I will join you?"

"That'd be great, Svetlana. I'll be right here."

She walked away while the gang got an eyeful. "Her English is worse than Vidu's," Jim said. "But her ass is a lot nicer."

"You can thank me after I get a lap dance and possibly more if I'm lucky." Blake froze in place as he got up from the table. "Shitballs."

"If it isn't my sister's punk-ass kid. Didn't think I'd miss my nephew's bachelor party, did ya?" A scraggly, mullet-haired man with a potbelly and a roguish grin approached the table.

It was Blake's uncle, Russ. The man was one part Al Bundy, one part Archie Bunker and three parts douchebag. Forty-five years old, Russ's binge drinking, three divorces and two bricks on his paycheck left him looking much older. "Who's catering this party, anyways?" He sat down uninvited, reeking of Old Spice and chewing tobacco.

"Margaritas are on special," Blake said flatly.

"That kind of drink will put some hair on your pussy. No, I'll take a Jack and Coke, and keep 'em coming."

Blake knew his uncle would be a tick on his ass for the rest of the night. What's worse, lending the parasite money was the only sure way to get rid of him.

Interrupting the family reunion, a middle-aged stripper with a long c-section scar approached the group. "Need company?" Her sunken lips betrayed the toothless smile of a meth-head.

"I could go for a gummy." Left-Nut pointed downwards.

"Come on, I need to make money. I lost my job last week and this is my first day here." This was obvious bullshit as the lady had the downtrodden look of a club veteran.

"Were you a dentist?"

She glared at Left-Nut. "Seriously, I have three kids to feed. Get a lap dance or at least buy me a drink."

Russ waved her away. "Bitch, I came here to forget my own problems, not learn about yours."

"I wasn't talking to you, cheap-ass."

Trent finally showed up as the stripper stormed off. The overweight cop waved his badge to avoid paying the cover charge and walked over. "You guys look fucked up." He surveyed their pitiful state and nodded at Russ. "Who invited Billy Ray Cyrus?"

"It's my Uncle Russ," Blake said sheepishly. "He's gonna be partying with us. I guess."

"That jagoff's your uncle?" Trent said then shrugged. "Anyways, who wants to buy some blow?"

Smokey, Blake and a few others followed Trent into the bathroom to kick things up a notch. While they blasted off, Charlie bounced some lies off Mike and settled on being a bestselling author who coached rugby on the side. Pretty standard bullshit.

Twenty minutes of booze and boobs later, a trampy woman in NASCAR gear approached the table. "This might sound weird, but my cousin wants to hook up tonight. It's her twenty-first, and she hasn't ever been with a man."

Left-Nut leaned forward, arching an eyebrow. "Now you're talkin' my language. Where is she?"

"That's her right there." The girl was rocking a Disney tank top, she had the faint hint of a mustache, a full unibrow and a very lazy eye.

"Shit, that girl's face could make a train take a dirt road," Uncle Russ said, clearly no diplomat.

Left-Nut was unfazed. "I'm intrigued. Sell me on it."

"What if I throw in ten bucks?" the woman said through rotten teeth.

"Done. Gentlemen, I bid you adieu." Left-Nut took off with the poor girl, a shit-eating grin plastered on his face.

"He's gotta be breaking some laws," Mike said.

Smokey nodded. "True, but the only cop in the building's selling coke in the bathroom."

"Not even the crack of dawn's safe around that boy," Russ said, clearly impressed.

Charlie ignored his idiot friend and focused on his own scandalous plans. He had to hand it to Blake: the guy was arrogant, but he sure made things happen.

"Are you going to bang this chick or what?" Smokey asked and Charlie shrugged.

"That girl screws random guys," Russ said and paused to light a generic cigarette. "I can tell."

Charlie hesitated to take Russ's advice since the man's reputation definitely preceded him. "How would you know?"

Russ leaned back as if lecturing schoolchildren. "You think you're first class pussy-hounds, but you guys don't know shit. She's burning a cigarette right now. She knows it'll kill her someday, but she does it anyways. Just like she knows fucking random dudes is bad for her. It's simple. If she smokes, she pokes." Impressed with himself, Russ ordered his nephew to buy him a shot of tequila.

"I hope for my sake you're right." Charlie said as he prepared for the encounter, but he'd temporarily forgotten about the presence of Trent – an infamous cock-blocker.

Of course, Trent had returned from the bathroom and was now making a move of his own on Svetlana. "Hey, sweetheart, what do you think about coming over for a little fun tonight? We're gonna have like a foot of snow." She looked confused, so Trent elaborated. "Coke, I mean a *lot* of coke." He always tried the direct approach.

Charlie's hackles rose as he realized Trent was trying to snake him, but Svetlana simply ignored the cop's advances. "Sorry, the professor and I are having nice conversation at my place." She took Charlie by the arm. "Ready?"

On their way out, Charlie gave Trent a wink and a knowing smile. He didn't get too many victories over his roommate and this one looked to be sweet indeed.

"Why the fuck did she call him the professor anyways?" Trent asked.

"It's his back story. But don't worry, that girl's out of your price range anyways," Blake said.

"No way, you mean she's a professional?"

Blake nodded. "I wanted to help Charlie out of his rut. He's been a real sad-sack lately."

"Does he know she's a hooker?"

"Not a clue."

"That's hilarious." Trent looked at his watch. "Speaking of skanks, we need to head home for the private show."

The remaining group assembled outside and began to catch various cabs while Russ stared at Mike for a few awkward seconds. "Hold on, I think I recognize you. Ain't you the one they call Faggot Bill or something?"

"It's Gay Mike, actually, but you can call me Mike."

"Okay, Gay Mike, let's share a ride. I'd like to get in on that private show the pig was talking about." Russ smiled and put his arm around Mike as if they were old friends. "You're gonna have to spot me though, I'm all outta cash."

Chapter 7
Two Ships Passing in the Night

Stretching out like a cat in a comfortable bed, Charlie yawned as he savored the memories of the night before. He then wrapped his arms around his sleeping partner and got ready for round two. But something was amiss. He didn't remember Svetlana's arms being so muscular, her skin so rough or her breath smelling like stale vodka and Cheetos.

"*Dzien dobry.*" An unexpectedly manly voice greeted Charlie. "Good morning."

His eyes shot open and he was instantly face to face with a stoutly built Polish goon. "It seems you owe me money?" the man asked, although it was more of a statement.

Charlie looked around and saw the girl making coffee in the kitchen. "What the hell's going on here, Svetlana?"

"That's not my name, idiot." Charlie wasn't the only one lying the night before.

To add insult to injury, she didn't look nearly as good without the effects of alcohol, bad lighting and an erection.

None of that mattered a second later when a meaty fist hammered Charlie's eye socket and sent him rolling out of bed and onto the hardwood floor, naked and dazed. He quickly grabbed his pants and hopped into them while backing away from the bed.

The other man rose and nonchalantly pulled out a switchblade as if he were about to carve an apple. "Your friend paid two hours," he said in broken English. "You stayed eight. So you owe me six hundred. *Gdzie są moje pieniądze?*" he yelled. "Where's my money?" The pimp soon advanced several feet and cut off the escape route through the front door.

Charlie stalled. "I can get the six hundred, no problem." Of course, there was a huge problem because the only things in his wallet were a maxed out credit card and the condom he should have used.

"You will take us to ATM?"

"Yeah, sure."

The thug's phone rang and he reached into his pocket, giving Charlie the opening he needed. Without hesitation, he dove out the window, bounced off the fire escape and tumbled down two flights of metal stairs. Polish curses and the sound of a loud bitch-slap to a hooker's mouth were all that followed, and Charlie ran off. He almost felt bad for the girl. Almost.

After cutting through alleyways and jumping a turnstile like a criminal, he boarded the Red Line train, shirtless, shoeless and bleeding, but alive. Actually, he hadn't felt this alive in years.

The train took off as Charlie grabbed a seat and caught his breath. He couldn't decide what pissed him off most — that Blake set him up, that he had sex with a hooker, or that some scumbag tried to rob him.

Charlie pulled his bare feet off the scum-covered floor and then shuddered, remembering what another body part had touched hours before. "Too bad I don't have health insurance," he said while checking his phone, which of course was dead.

A nearby door opened and two hoodie-wearing youths swaggered in like royalty surveying their kingdom. They were the type that asked a person for change then bashed their head in with a brick. Real winners.

Charlie instinctively tensed up before he realized he had nothing left to lose. Besides, he looked like a homeless crack head, and nobody bothered messing with them.

An Asian businessman in a tailored suit, however, was another story. He had been motionless for a few minutes except for coughing, and the sweaty man looked to be coming down from a heroin binge. Easy pickings.

One of the delinquents poked the man, causing him to rock forward and projectile vomit onto the thug's spotless white sneakers. "Motherfucker!" His friend giggled, setting the youth off even more. "You're gonna pay for that, bitch."

Charlie bolted when the train reached the next stop, having already had his day's fill of random violence. Sure enough, a guttural scream erupted as the doors shut, and he turned to watch the brawl. But it was the teenager banging on the door as the train pulled away, his face pressed against the window. Even stranger, the boy's eyes had the desperation of a wild animal caught in a trap.

"Dude must have known karate," Charlie said while starting his long walk home, tired and barefoot. That change of scenery Jim had mentioned sounded better and better.

Chapter 8
Hookers and Hangovers

A Steely Dan ringtone competed with the chorus of snores in the apartment for several minutes before Trent rose to answer. The commotion had roused the semi-conscious Russ, who was sleeping in the bathtub of all places. "Shut that shit off," he said with a whine and curled back up with the towels he'd used for blankets.

Trent wanted to ignore the call, but several collection agencies and a gambling problem meant the eight-year veteran needed overtime.

He cleared the phlegm from his throat. "Talk to me." There was yelling on the other end. "You know I'm off today?" Trent replied, and there was more yelling. "Fine. Pick me up in ten." He hung up, wondering why they had to send someone to get him.

Vidu glanced at his knockoff watch and sat up. He'd promised to see a friend run a five-k through Bucktown and was about to miss it. The woman actually gave him the time of day, and Vidu planned to ask her out as a last ditch effort to find a wife.

The Sri Lankan found the remains of the bachelor party in the living room, and it wasn't pretty. Trent's strippers had failed to show up, and the night ended with a whimper instead of a bang. His friends were now sprawled in all directions, and the unmistakably sour smell of vomit wafted through the air. The place was a real pigsty of spilled beer, Mexican takeout, buzzing flies and cigarette butts. It was just like college.

"Anyone want to come see the race? It's down the street."

Left-Nut sat up in a La-Z Boy. "You know I don't miss girls in spandex."

Vidu sighed. "Does anyone *else* want to come?"

"Yeah, I'll go," Jim said. "This place is nasty, and Cindy won't be here until noon. We can grab breakfast too."

Trent swaggered in carrying a Gatorade in one hand and his nightstick in the other. "You boners have fun. I'm going to work."

"I thought you were off?" Vidu said.

"There's a riot or something on the Southside. Sounds like a level three chimp out to me. But I'm getting time and a half today so screw it. Plus I might get to bust some skulls."

"Be careful out there," Jim said.

"Don't worry about me." Nobody was. "Worry about any Mondays that get in my way." Trent swung his nightstick for emphasis.

Vidu was confused by the term. "What's a Monday?"

Trent laughed. "A black person, you know?"

"Why do you call them Mondays?" Vidu's eyes narrowed.

"Because everybody hates Mondays, duh."

"Asshole," Jim said. "But we need to get going."

"Fucking racist," Vidu mumbled under his breath as he walked past the cop.

Trent rubbed Vidu's hair. "Ah, lighten up cupcake. You camel jockeys are too serious."

"I'm from southeast Asia, idiot. You know it's covered with rainforests right?"

"You're all sand-humpers in my book." Trent was an equal opportunity offender.

Like most conversations with the cop, this one ended on a bad note as the trio walked down the rickety porch and headed out, eager for some fresh air.

*   *   *

Charlie's feet ached something awful as he neared home. The former track standout paused to rub them and noticed his growing beer belly. "Better get those running shoes this week," he said as the front door burst open and several of his friends filed out. He'd been making that promise for two years.

"Talking to yourself is a sign of madness," Jim said and then noticed Charlie's growing shiner. "Whoa man, what happened to you?"

"Some homeless pricks rolled me," Charlie said while doing his best to avoid eye contact. "They tried to take my wallet but I got away."

"Was this before or after they took your shirt and shoes?" Left-Nut reached for the tender flesh underneath Charlie's right eye only to have his hand slapped away.

Vidu didn't have time for small talk. "Come to the race and tell us all about it."

"I'll pass. I've got a monster headache, and my hangover hasn't even started yet."

"It smells like assholes and tacos in there. Come on," Vidu said, his patience waning.

"And there's bound to be plenty of ladies at the race," Left-Nut added.

But Charlie couldn't think about women considering what he'd just gone through. Still, he didn't want to start cleaning and knew Trent wouldn't lift a finger, so he grabbed sandals from the porch and borrowed Jim's over shirt. Moments later, they started the four-block hike down Damon Street, past tiny cafés and overpriced boutiques. It was a beautiful morning.

Despite his best efforts, nobody bought Charlie's story. "Okay... did you get lucky with the Euro-trash or what?" Jim said.

Charlie searched for plausible deniability on the hooker aspect of the story. "We went back to her place and talked. She's a sweet girl, wants to be a writer someday."

"I know the type," Jim said. "They work at strip clubs by night and do award winning screenplays by day. You know, I think Vidu got a lap dance from an up and coming economist."

"She knew how to count money," Vidu said.

Charlie ignored his friends. "She's new to the country and working her way through—"

"Cut the shit, we know you nailed her," Left-Nut said and stopped walking.

Charlie was too tired to put up much of a defense, and they weren't going to drop the issue. "Fine. Yeah, I nailed her. We did it five times, once in the shower and once on the kitchen table. I even gave her a Bullwinkle. Happy?"

Jim looked horrified. "I knew you were hard up, but I never thought you'd stoop to hookers. Oh how the mighty have fallen."

"How did you know?"

"Blake told us he felt sorry for you," Jim explained. "Said he'd get you laid even if he had to pay for it."

Charlie's blood boiled. Blake had gotten him roughed up and made him look like a pathetic loser. But with no way to deny it, he decided to go the deflection route and turned the tables on his white-haired friend. "Why are you all harassing me? At least I didn't bang an invalid."

Left-Nut had a moronic smile plastered on his face. "What's your point?"

"My point is I might have fucked a hooker last night, but you *became* one when you prosti-tarded yourself out."

"Yeah it was crazy," Left-Nut replied, then paused for dramatic effect. "I would have done it for free."

"As for what happened to me? I had no idea she was a hooker. For real."

Even Vidu snickered. "You thought a hot chick threw herself at you in a strip club? And *I'm* gullible?"

"Look, I didn't know, and I certainly didn't know Blake only paid for two hours. Some guy, I guess it was her pimp, woke me up and wanted six hundred bucks. I'd already spent all my money at the club."

"Ignoring the fact that you don't have that much money anyways, what did you do?" Jim asked

"The guy blasted me in the face and then whipped out a knife, so I jumped through the window and fell down the fire escape."

"Which is why you have no shoes, right?" Left-Nut asked. "Nice escape. Reminds me of the time—"

"Yeah, it was intense," Charlie said. "But to top it off, I just saw a banker on the train beat up some gangbangers."

Left-Nut stirred the pot. "Nobody gives a shit about punks on the train. Are you going to get even with Blake?"

"I might give him one of these," Charlie said and pointed to his eye.

Left-Nut shrugged. "You can't be too mad, he did get you laid after all."

"Speaking of which, I hope you both bagged up last night," Jim said as the group resumed their walk.

Charlie shook his head and Left-Nut laughed. "What is this, junior high? Of course not."

"You guys are complete idiots. I swear your dicks are gonna fall right off."

"I think it's funny Charlie got beat up after everyone laughed at me," Vidu said.

Charlie rolled his eyes. "Have you ever won a fight?"

"Of course. Remember the junior year Tahiti Party?" Vidu brought up an annual festival where college kids wore swimsuits and straw hats, drank alcoholic punch and swallowed goldfish whole.

"You mean your throw down with the theatre kid?" Charlie asked.

"Yes. That guy was like a mongoose."

"That wasn't exactly Clash of the Titans," Jim said. "It was more like a blind Urkel fighting a gay Screech."

"Whatever. Your wife probably beats you for putting the toilet roll on backwards. That nonsense wouldn't happen in my country because the man is the boss."

"It wouldn't happen in your country because nobody ever uses toilet paper," Jim quipped.

The griping and sniping continued until the friends reached the finish line of the race. Packs of runners came down the blockaded street while a group of bored spectators milled about. Vidu rudely pushed his way to the front, wanting his crush, Julia, to hear his encouragement.

The others hung near the back of the crowd and waited. And waited, and waited. Finally, a chubby girl with an awkward running style approached to a round of applause from the crowd. "Go, Julia!" Vidu yelled, startling a few bystanders with the surprising volume of his voice. "You can do it, you're almost there."

Julia found him in the crowd of faces and gave a wave and a very nice smile. Charlie was surprised at how cute she was, but he was even more surprised when a figure darted from the crowd and tackled her like a linebacker, driving the woman's soft body onto the pavement. It was madness.

Vidu instantly sprang forward and threw a punch like never before, somehow connecting with the assailant's jaw. He reached back to throw another haymaker and then looked at his hand in horror to find two of his fingers were bloody stumps. Another man dragged Vidu to the ground while a third and then fourth violently piled on. The used car salesman disappeared into the tangle of arms and legs and screams.

Chapter 9
Shit Meets Fan

Trent flicked his cigarette into the rose bushes and lit another. As he savored the chalky menthol flavor, two ambulances streaked by with lights flashing and horns blaring. He'd been waiting for his ride for fifteen minutes and wondered what in the hell was going on.

A squad car finally pulled up. "I'm driving," Trent told the attractive woman scowling from behind the wheel.

"We really don't have time for your macho bullshit," the woman replied sharply.

He got in while his ex-partner, Sarah Birdsong, avoided eye contact and pulled away. The descendant of Sioux Indians had a fiery disposition and pissed Trent off slightly more than she turned him on. Slightly.

"Put that out. You know I'm allergic."

"Jesus, you're like my mother," he said and tossed it out the window. "Only my mother never gave me crabs."

Sarah slammed on the brakes. "Let's get this straight. Sleeping with you was the biggest mistake of my life, and you're an asshole for taking advantage of me."

"You weren't that drunk, sunshine."

"Bullshit. But we need to set that aside for now."

"And why's that?" Trent asked.

Sarah's voice faltered. "Something big's going down."

Trent leaned forward. "I'm listening. Fucking Al-Qaeda, isn't it?"

"Loads of people are getting really sick." A 10-101 call came across the squad radio, code for a civil disturbance.

"I wondered why they sent a car," Trent said.

"Every cop in town's been called up."

His fear turned to anger. "We aren't trained for this. I spend my time harassing teenagers and sleeping behind abandoned factories."

"FEMA's in charge and the National Guard's doing the heavy lifting. They're running a triage at the United Center, and we have to man roadblocks. No one gets in or out. No one. We've got live-fire orders here."

"Do we get masks or something? I mean, what's gonna keep us from getting sick?"

"They don't think it's airborne so we're not supposed to let anyone get too close," she said. "Whatever it is, they think it's spreading by direct contact."

Trent was sick to his stomach, and even felt a little ashamed that Sarah was handling the situation so well. He wondered if maybe she wasn't as useless as he'd been telling everyone.

Sarah grabbed his shoulder. "A lot of people are depending on us. Are you ready?"

He nodded and lit another Parliament while thinking about the woman sitting next to him. Trent didn't actually hate her, but rejection always made him act like a junior-high bully. For her part, Sarah did find him charming in his own uncouth sort of way, and she hadn't been that drunk. But she would never admit it.

New calls flooded in as the car picked up speed. First, there was a 10-46, sick person and ambulance en route, followed by a 10-54, possible dead body. Codes 20 and 10-57 meant an officer needed assistance and shots had been fired. They grew even worse from there.

"Wow, the shit's hitting the fan. It's like a full moon on steroids," Trent said and then changed his tone. "Sarah, look... I just gotta say... I've been a complete prick."

"Now isn't the time—"

"No, now is the time. From here on out, you get nothing but respect from me."

Her pouty lips flashed a tempting smile. "Thanks. You know, I..." A heavy object shattered the windshield and

Sarah instinctively slammed on the brakes, quickly losing control. The car only stopped after jumping the curb and crumpling around a telephone pole.

"I knew I should have drove," Trent muttered as he fought the darkness creeping over him. Two long minutes later, an intense pain jolted him awake. The lit cigarette had landed on his lap and the smoldering cherry slowly burned through his slacks and into his flesh.

Meanwhile, a warm and wet liquid ran down Trent's face and momentarily blinded him while a strange clicking noise came from somewhere nearby. He patted the flames out and then rubbed his eyes, blinking for a few seconds. The world slowly came into focus, as did the cause of the clicking sound.

"Jesus Christ!"

Confronting Trent was some grade-A nightmare fuel. An old lady was stuck in the windshield mere inches from his face, chomping and drooling like a ravenous beast. The woman pressed further into the windshield, ignoring the broken shards slicing into her neck. Blood and spit dripped onto Trent's forehead like Chinese water torture as he fumbled with his pistol. He aimed the shaking sidearm at the woman's shattered face while reaching a hand out to Sarah's shoulder.

Trent shook her, slowly at first, then like a rag-doll. "Wake up!"

Sarah mumbled incoherently, so he smacked her, hard, and she slowly came to. "What happened?"

"Woman driver. And your airbag didn't go off so don't move. I'm coming around to get you." Trent eased the door open and put one foot on the ground. Dull and empty eyes followed him from the windshield.

The old woman jerked her head backwards and Trent scrambled out to raise his firearm. But the freak-show was hopelessly stuck. She gave one final furious tug before her head popped right off, making a disgusting ripping noise in the process. The corpse slumped to the ground, twitched for a few agonizing seconds, and then lay still.

Blaaaaugh. Trent threw up the super-nachos he ate at four a.m. as well as several confiscated pain pills. He wiped his face and turned to Sarah. "Are you hurt?"

"Yeah, I think it's bad." She coughed up blood. "My leg hurts like hell."

Trent could see a pure white bone poking through her pant leg and realized it was a nasty compound fracture. He grabbed the radio. "Unit 145 has an officer down near Hermitage and Augusta, ambulance needed." There was no reply so he repeated himself four times. "Somebody fucking pick up!" Still no answer. Other than a figure approaching from the south, the street was oddly deserted. "Sit tight, we got someone running towards us."

"I'm not..." She coughed up more bright blood. "...going anywhere."

Trent waited until the man was twenty yards out and raised his pistol. The runner, a black man wearing a janitor's outfit, gestured to Trent to lower his weapon. He did and the man cautiously approached, sweating heavily and gasping for air.

"Thank God. I thought I was all alone. You got to get me outta here," he said between breaths.

"Back up, buddy. Why are you running?" Trent raised his gun again.

"I work down at Cook County Hospital. It's going crazy down there. Man, we need to go."

"What do you mean?" Trent asked.

"The hospital was packed, but more people kept showing up and we couldn't let anyone else in. Then folks started going ghetto and it got nuts. People were screaming, punching, they were even biting each other."

"You ran off?"

"Hell yeah I did. My friend got his damn ear bit off right in front of me. I wasn't gonna wait for the bus."

"Then what?" Trent asked.

"It spilled into the streets and then big trucks showed up. There was a bunch of gunshots."

"Military?"

"Fuck, how many questions are you gonna ask?" Trent glared, so the man continued. "I hear gunshots all the time, and I ain't never heard any like that. They were shooting at everything."

Trent grabbed the radio. "Where is everybody? I got an officer down. Hello?"

"Look, I ain't sticking around. There were some dudes chasing me and I don't know where they are." He finally noticed the decapitated body in the street. "Holy shit. You hit that bitch with your car?"

At that moment, a group of subway workers, several bums and a naked man rounded the corner two blocks away. They moved with a strange shambling gait, almost as if they were drunk.

"Those are the guys."

Trent ignored him. "She's hurt, so we'll need to move her till help comes."

"We? You got a turd in your pocket? I mean, I ain't doing nothing but getting outta here."

"Listen, asshole—"

"It ain't asshole, it's Tyrone."

Trent cocked the hammer back on his pistol. "Listen, Tyrone, I'm not asking you."

"Fine, but don't think I won't sue your ass," Tyrone replied. "Police motherfucking brutality, that's what this is. I'll get Jesse Jackson up in here."

"You can take every penny I have, brother. But we need to get her into one of these buildings. Be careful, her leg is busted and probably her ribs too." Trent put his leather wallet into Sarah's mouth and gently eased the door open. So far so good. Even better, the crowd hadn't noticed them.

Sarah clamped down and fought the urge to pass out as they started to pull. But the shattered femur worked a jagged groove through her thigh and blood quickly pooled on the floor.

"She's bleeding too much, we gotta put her back," Trent said and gritted his teeth. They carefully eased her into the front seat.

As luck would have it, the radio crackled back to life. "What's your location again unit 145?" Trent and Tyrone looked to each other then turned back to the crowd that was now numbering in the dozens and staring directly at the car.

Tyrone chose that instant to flee, and the crowd surged towards them while Trent froze. Looking at his partner, he noticed her beauty even under extreme pain, and as the morning sun glistened off Sarah's tear-soaked, emerald eyes, he knew what he should do. He knew what he must do. And he did the exact opposite.

"Don't leave me!" Sarah shouted as Trent took off. The mob reached the car and several forms dove through the window while the rest followed their moving prey.

Ghastly screams echoed off the buildings followed by the sharp crack of a pistol. Trent simply quickened his pace and put Sarah Birdsong behind him, figuratively and literally. A few minutes later his gut ached, his lungs burned and the crowd grew closer by the step.

Meanwhile, Tyrone had problems of his own. Already winded, his ill-fitting work boots were causing his feet to blister. Still, he was pulling away from the overweight cop.

Trent's years of chain-smoking hadn't given him much to work with, and he soon hit the wall as his silent chasers closed in. So Trent stopped running and fired every round in his clip. The first shot grazed Tyrone's shoulder and the second blew the man's knee apart.

"You son of a bitch!"

The janitor hit the pavement and Trent didn't even turn around to see the mob rip the helpless man to pieces. He was only a mile from home and just might make it after all.

Chapter 10
Par for the Course

Charlie and Jim made their way towards the dog pile while the crowd panicked and spectators ran in every direction. Fights were breaking out all over, and Left-Nut, being Left-Nut, had already fled amidst the pandemonium.

Reaching the scrum and seeing Vidu's orange shirt at the bottom of the pile, Charlie grabbed his squirming legs and pulled him from the mass of tangled bodies. Vidu slid out and latched onto a lady running past, tripping and grabbing her in one fluid motion. He opened his mouth wide and ripped a chunk of flesh from the screaming woman's calf.

"What the fuck are you doing?" Charlie dropped his friend and backed away in horror as two more deranged lunatics tore into the woman's trembling body like she was a downed wildebeest.

Jim tugged at Charlie's arm and they sprinted pell-mell towards the apartment, ignoring the trampled and torn apart bodies around them. Men and women, young and old, found themselves caught in the quickly growing cycle of exponential carnage. If there could be hell on earth, it would look a lot like this.

They caught up with Left-Nut and told him to pick up the pace with a few choice words. One hot minute later, the trio reached the apartment. Of course, Charlie had lost the key during his tumble down the fire escape earlier, and the doorbell was broken.

After they pounded on the door for what would seem like an eternity, Smokey emerged wearing a zebra-patterned

Snuggie and holding a joint. "Who kicked your ass?" he said upon seeing his friend's shiner.

Charlie shoved Smokey aside, slammed the door and turned the deadbolt. "Everybody wake the fuck up!"

The remaining crew was in varying states of disarray, but the consensus was that nobody wanted to "wake the fuck up."

Blake rubbed the sleep from his eyes while sitting up on the couch. "This better be good, my head's pounding." He squinted. "Holy shit, Charlie, what happened to your face?"

"Guys, something crazy's going on and I'm not kidding."

"Like what?" Mike asked. "Terrorists?"

Charlie shook his head. "I got no clue, but it's a fucking nightmare outside."

"It's true, people are going ape-shit," Jim added while a speechless Left-Nut nodded in agreement.

Russ crossed his arms. "You guys think you can pull one over on old Russ do you? Well you can all kiss my ass because I'm not taking the bait."

Charlie pulled the living room drapes back and revealed the spiraling mayhem in the neighborhood. "Take a look for yourself." Cars zipped past, ignoring traffic signals and common sense as people ran about in a panic.

"Okay, let's see this crazy nightmare," Russ said with finger quotations as he brushed past Charlie. When he got to the window, a speeding ice cream truck crashed into a fire hydrant and sent water shooting straight into the air. "Damn, they're giving that truck driver the Reginald Denny treatment. Wait, are they... are they fuckin' eating that guy?" The truck's tune continued to play during the assault.

"We need to stay inside," Blake said, stating the obvious.

"Where's Vidu?" Mike asked.

Jim looked at the floor. "He didn't make it."

"What do you mean he didn't make it?"

"I mean he's running around biting people and shit," Jim said. "He didn't make it."

Blake turned on the news while others tried to call loved ones and Charlie did a head count. "Who are we missing?"

"Trent's at work, so only Big Rob," Blake said.

Jim was puzzled. "He was supposed to stay here till I took him to the train station."

Smokey put his joint out in an empty beer can. "He was complaining that you wouldn't let him use the toilet. You don't think—"

"I know exactly where he is," Charlie said and headed for the front door.

*　　*　　*

Smokey's elderly downstairs tenant stared out her front window at the man sleeping blissfully in her rosebushes. Making matters worse, the giant's pants were around his ankles, exposing himself to the world. After getting no help from the police, Mrs. Stone planned to use her garden hose on the delinquent.

Meanwhile, Charlie crept down the front stairs and found Big Rob right where he expected. "You gotta wake up," he said and tapped his friend's forehead.

Rob rolled over, revealing definite morning wood and the true origins of his nickname. "Where am I?"

Her sensibilities were now completely overwhelmed, and Mrs. Stone ran outside screaming like a banshee. "Out of my yard, you sodomites!"

Charlie grabbed his aged neighbor by the shoulders and forcefully shoved her into the apartment. "Get inside, you old bitch," he said while shutting the door. "Pull your pants up and come on. I don't have time to explain."

But no one ever talked to Mrs. Stone like that, and they definitely didn't put their hands on her either. The feisty grandmother of twelve and former WWII riveter calmly grabbed her dead husband's Big Bertha golf club from the entryway and crept back outside.

Rob was taking his sweet time and turned his head to the street. "Ooh, I hear the ice-cream man."

Charlie pulled Rob up by the ear. "I'm not kidding, you need to hurry up and—" Charlie's sentence ended abruptly as a wooden driver smashed the back of his skull and knocked him to his knees. It saved his life.

At that exact moment, a sprinting maniac sailed right over him and crashed into the furious granny. It instantly began to savage the old-firecracker, although she did get a few good whacks in.

Now Rob had no trouble moving quickly and even beat Charlie upstairs where Jim held the door open, slamming it as they entered. "Dumbass," he said and gave Rob a hug.

The friends gathered in the living room and tried to make sense of the lunacy, but it was difficult to focus with random screams and the ice cream song blaring outside.

"Has anyone been able to call out yet?" Charlie asked.

"Everything's busy," Blake said as he tried in vain to call his fiancée again. "Must be too many calls overloading the system, like on nine-eleven."

There was a loud pounding on the front door, and time seemed to stand still. "Somebody order a pizza?" Blake's uncle said with a nervous laugh.

Charlie peeked out the window overlooking the second-story porch. "You gotta be kidding me, it's Mrs. Stone." The nonagenarian wasn't looking too good either as she was missing an eye and a good chunk of her scalp. Still, she methodically hammered away at the steel door, leaving behind a trail of bloody handprints.

"Now we're getting attacked by senior citizens," Cliff said in amazement. "What's next, killer midgets?"

Rob put one hand up to his ear. "Anyone hear that?" A faint cracking noise came from Trent's bedroom. They rushed in to see rocks hitting the window.

Charlie stuck his head outside and found an exhausted Trent hiding behind old furniture in the alleyway.

The cop waved up. "It's about goddamn time." He looked downwards. "Ah man, I stepped in a huge pile of shit." Big Rob grimaced, knowing where it came from.

"Go to the back door," Charlie said.

Trent gave the dirtiest of dirty looks. "I'm not a fucking moron, I already tried that. There's a bunch of assholes sniffing around out back like they're here for a barbecue. Just get the old bag off the porch."

"Okay, wait here," Charlie said and ran upstairs with Big Rob close behind.

There was a huge crash out front, and Trent peeked around the corner to see blood streaming off the porch.

A fifty-pound air conditioner picks up terminal velocity very quickly, and the widow found this out the hard way when one landed on her head and crunched her frail bones like an accordion. Big Rob waved down from the roof. The coast was clear.

Chapter 11
Shock and Awesome

The next few minutes were tension filled as the local news kept reporting on a street festival and the phone issues continued. Even text messages weren't working.

Smokey opened his laptop to find some answers. "The *Drudge Report* says there's a race riot on the Southside, and they're calling in the National Guard. They think it's a protest over the new prison."

"Typical liberal media bullshit," Russ added.

"A protest? Blake said. "Doesn't look like any I've ever seen, you know, Code Pink whackos and Occupy Wall Street fucktards."

"It could be anything at this point," Mike said. "Mass hysteria, biological weapons or—"

"Vidu had this weird look on his face like he... like he was possessed," Jim said.

Charlie had a rare epiphany. "I bet the sick guy on the train had something to do with this, the one that went after the punks. I mean, what are the odds?"

"If you're right, it's gonna be all over Chicago," Mike added. "Unless someone was smart enough to shut down the trains, and I doubt it. Which means they'll quarantine the whole damned city."

Charlie approached Trent, who had remained curiously silent. "What did they say at work?"

"The police don't know shit. I was supposed to set up roadblocks by the United Center, and we didn't even make it there."

"Did they tell you anything?" Charlie said.

Trent shook his head. "Like I said, they didn't know jack. We were supposed to follow FEMA and the Guard, end of story." He was clearly hiding something.

Finally, the local studio cut in with a direct feed. "This is Tom Clinton of Channel Seven and we're coming to you live from Chicago with some important breaking news."

"About time," Left-Nut said, now wearing a shirt wrapped around his face like a surgical mask. "It's the end of the world and these morons have been covering a flea market in Logan Square."

"We've gotten scattered reports from across the city about a possible avian flu outbreak. The CDC and Mayor's office are ordering Chicago residents to stay indoors. I repeat, stay indoors. This virus appears to be more dangerous than the 2009 H1N1 strain and is highly contagious."

"I thought it was a riot, now bird flu? They expect us to believe that?" Charlie bounced an empty can off the screen.

"We're asking you to remain calm. Most importantly, do not attempt to flee the city. The roads are too dangerous at this time, and you will be jailed if apprehended. If you see someone acting erratically, avoid them at all costs."

"And there it is," Mike said as his eyes teared up. "That means it's a quarantine situation. We're trapped."

The reporter listened to his earpiece as sweat trickled down his forehead and onto the table. "We're now getting word that air traffic has been grounded for both O'Hare and Midway airports. There's also been a report of a large explosion at the Six Rivers Nuclear Facility in Missouri. We have no indication that the two situations are related in any way." The live feed blinked out and was replaced by a technical difficulties screen and horrible elevator music.

"Arma-fuckin-geddon," Russ said as he cracked open a cold one, deciding to face this day like he had every day for the past thirty years. Shit-faced.

"Turn on some real news," Blake said.

"Don't have cable," Charlie replied. His head throbbed as the adrenaline wore off, so he snuck a vicodin from Trent's stash and chased it with a pull of Captain Morgan.

"What about a radio?" Cliff asked.

"Do you think I look like Jed Clampett?" Charlie said. "Everything's digital now."

Meanwhile, chaos reigned outside as roving marauders took down pedestrians and snatched people from cars in an orgy of primal violence. It was almost fascinating, in a strange, voyeuristic way, to see society crumbling down, and Charlie wondered if maybe Russ was right. Maybe it *was* Armageddon.

Still unable to reach his pregnant wife, Jim started to crack. "I've got to go," he said and headed for the door.

Charlie blocked his way. "You know you won't make it twenty feet out there. We just need to sit tight and wait for more information."

"You wouldn't be doing Cindy any favors running off half-cocked and getting yourself killed," Mike said and put his hand on Jim's shoulder. This would normally be where someone made fun of Mike's choice of words, but this was no time for jokes. "They're probably all locked away at Jen's condo," he added.

Blake nodded. "The place is pretty secure. It's on the second floor, so they should be somewhat safe."

"What's that mean, somewhat?" Jim's, voice rose. "This is my wife we're talking about here... *and* my child." He looked at Blake. "And we're talking about your fiancée for god's sake." Next, he turned to Bruce. "Your girlfriend's there too, buddy."

"I've only been dating her about six months so..." Bruce's face turned red and there was an awkward silence with only the ever-present ice-cream truck song blasting in the background.

Finally, the anchor reappeared on screen. "I apologize, but we seem to have things back in order. That being said, we're going live to Caitlyn Sanders outside Wrigley Field."

A short brunette began speaking. "Tom, today's game has been cancelled, and people are exiting behind me, many using shirts as improvised face masks."

"That's only two miles north of here," Charlie said.

"The fans are leaving quickly and in an orderly manner, and there's been no—" She looked off camera for a moment, then kicked off her high heels and ran away.

"That's not good," Left-Nut said.

The cameraman whirled around and focused on a handful of people swiftly coming towards him, a dirty-looking guy in a Cubs uniform taking the lead. Before the cameraman could even take a step away, they were upon him, biting, ripping and tearing. He let out a blood-curdling scream as the camera hit the ground, tilting to show fluffy clouds slowly billowing by.

The shot returned to the newsroom and caught the speechless anchor in a state of utter shock. Blake couldn't believe his eyes either. "Holy shit, that was the bum who's always outside the ballgames. I'd recognize him anywhere, it's Ronnie Woo Woo."

"I'm not quite sure what we've just seen... you know what, screw this." The anchorman undid his microphone and stormed off the set while the technical difficulties screen appeared again. Channel Seven's final broadcast was over.

"That was live, so the little bird flu story ain't gonna fly anymore," Russ said and cracked open another beer, proud of his little witticism.

Mike fidgeted with his phone. "I wish Twitter was still working. I could have a tweet for the ages right now."

"Twitter? Is that what you do to your boyfriend's balls on his birthday?" Russ said and belched loudly. He seemed to actually be enjoying himself.

Someone banged at the front door again, and Rob ran to the window. "Two more on the porch."

Smokey mashed his keyboard in frustration. "Now the internet's down."

"That's it, I'm going," Jim said. "Who's coming with me?"

Blake sighed. "I guess I am."

"I'm in," Cliff said and scowled as the others remained seated. "Pussies." He looked at Blake. "Now you see who your real friends are."

"What do we do?" Blake asked. "We can't just stroll out of here."

"My Lexus is right across the street, and we can blast our way out." Cliff revealed a ridiculously small pistol strapped to his leg. "I started packing when I got mugged after a Sox game."

Smokey produced a rusty-looking Saturday night special of his own. "Mine's bigger than yours."

"Why the hell do you have a gun?" Charlie asked.

"Duh, I'm a drug dealer," Smokey said and handed the pistol to Jim. "Good luck, bro."

"That's not a gun," Russ said with a horrible Australian accent while whipping out a huge revolver tucked between his belt and an overhanging beer belly. "Now, that's a gun." He tossed the clunky weapon to his nephew and then pulled a second one out dramatically. "And don't you worry, Uncle Russ always parties with twins."

Charlie shook his head. "You guys know it's illegal to have guns in the city right? And why do you have two?"

"I hauled gravel before my license got yanked, and every now and then I had to fend off the lot lizards. And it turned out a shit-load were trannies. They're a lot stronger than they look," he added with a knowing nod.

Mike wasn't convinced. "Okay, penis measurements and butchered *Crocodile Dundee* references aside, it's still a dumb idea. You'll have to drive through a freaking warzone out there, and the girls are probably safer where they are anyways."

"Save it, I'm going," Jim said.

Charlie saw the fire in Jim's eyes and knew he wouldn't be able to change his mind. "Fine, go. But be careful."

Russ chugged another beer then crumpled the can on his forehead while cocking the hammer back on his revolver. "Enough talk, let's roll." He opened the front window. "I'll clear the porch, you guys make a break for it."

Jim and Blake waited behind Cliff like a gang ready to shoot their way out of a Wild West bank. Russ gave several fake military hand signals and then leaned out and took aim at an elderly man wearing a bad hairpiece. "Hey, shitbird," he said and fired once, blasting off the top of the man's head and leaving the toupee hanging in midair for a split second like a bloody, levitating muskrat.

Russ didn't have long to admire his bull's-eye because the second man, a teenaged basketball player, launched himself off the railing and soared through the air with his mouth agape and arms outstretched. Uncle Russ backed up, but the crazed teen got a solid handful of hair while plummeting towards the ground. He took the cussing truck driver right along with him.

Rob and Mike somehow latched onto Russ's legs before he completely flew out the window. Still, the kid held tight and actually began to climb up Russ's mullet, Rapunzel style. Something had to give, and a with a sickening Velcro sound, part of Russ's feathery Kentucky waterfall peeled right off, taking the scalp and leaving behind a gushing wound. The teen crashed onto the sidewalk below and shattered both legs while crumpling into a heap. Unfazed, it crawled back towards the stairwell with Russ's bloody locks in hand.

Charlie yelled at his wavering friends to go as the others pulled a stunned Russ into the living room. Cliff led the charge outside, pausing to fire a round into the head of the crawling freak show and killing it instantly. They reached the car and peeled out, running over two snarling women and swerving onto the sidewalk to avoid a string of burning vehicles. Moments later, they had disappeared around the corner with a gang of runners trailing behind them and one clinging precariously to the hood.

"That certainly could have gone better," Left-Nut said while Russ held a can of beer to his raw scalp, letting loose a string of vulgarity unmatched in its content and sincerity.

Charlie had the sudden urge to relieve his bladder and ran to the bathroom where it felt like he literally pissed razor blades. "That whore," he mumbled to himself, and came back to the living room, wondering what else could possibly happen.

A nervous Mike cleared his throat loudly to capture his friends' attention. "I guess now's as good a time as any. Guys, I'm gay."

Chapter 12
Revelations and
Restraining Orders

Given their dire predicament, Mike's blockbuster news should have been no big deal. It should have been.

"How many times did you stare at my junk in the locker room? I should kick your ass on principle," Trent said as he puffed up, his bigotry not limited to racial lines.

"You're not my type, buddy," Mike responded. "Besides, I didn't know back then."

"I remember you banging chicks on spring break," Left-Nut said. "In fact, I hid in the closet a few times."

Charlie's patience was gone. "Is this a burning concern right now? Who gives a shit?"

"What are we gonna call him? He's been Gay Mike for years and we sure can't call him that now, it seems kinda mean," Big Rob said.

"How about Straight Mike," Left-Nut volunteered.

"Call me whatever you want, I thought I'd level with you. There's no reason not to at this point." He looked at Left-Nut. "And take that shirt off your head, you look like an idiot."

Smokey stood up and began rubbing his hands together. "As long as we're clearing the air..."

"Oh great. I suppose you're a homo, too?" Trent asked.

"Dude, not cool," Smokey said and gave him a dirty look. "But anyways... how do I put this?" He stumbled around the issue for a bit and then focused. "I'm a phony. I never actually sold my art like I told everyone."

"What about the pictures of the auction, the ones with you and Sean Penn?" Charlie said.

"Photoshopped from the Oscars. I added myself in and you can see Quentin Tarantino in the background if you look hard."

"Then how did you afford this place?" Blake asked. "It's not like you have a job, and you've always smoked more pot than you sold."

"Simple. I won the lottery a few years ago and didn't tell anyone. Two million and change. It's just my luck, now the world's ending. Ironic, huh?"

Charlie was dumbfounded. "You're a millionaire and you borrowed money from me last week? You let me go to that shit job every day to pay rent when you had all that cash? I'm gonna fucking kill you!"

Rob held Charlie back as Smokey tried to explain. "I wanted people to think I was successful."

"Nobody thought you were successful," Charlie said. "You've been stoned for the past fifteen years. Jackass."

"Besides, I'm not a millionaire anymore. I spent a ton retrofitting this place. Plus I have an expensive habit."

"Big deal. We could have been knee-deep in hookers and coke," Trent said.

"Be thankful this place is off the grid," Smokey said. "That means we'll have power no matter what happens."

"Actually, good job." Charlie calmed down as he realized Smokey was right. "I take back every snide hippy comment I ever made about you. Still, you could have hooked a brother up."

"You would've been as lazy as me, and weren't you just complaining about not having any direction in your life?" Charlie nodded, and Smokey continued. "And, Trent, what would have happened if we spent all that money partying?"

"I suppose we'd be dead. Not that it matters now. At least we wouldn't be dealing with this shit."

"It comes down to being prepared. A prudent person foresees danger and takes precautions. The simpleton goes blindly on and suffers the consequences. Proverbs 27:12."

"I didn't realize you were a bible thumper," Trent said.

"I'm not," Smokey said. "I got that from Armageddon Week on the History Channel. You'd be surprised to know how much television I watch."

Charlie scoffed. "Not really."

A sudden hail of gunfire somewhere in the neighborhood interrupted the conversation. "Sounds like M-16 bursts," Trent said. "Must be the National Guard." The shots ended as quickly as they began.

Moments later, Russ got a call through. "Everybody shut up for a second."

The plague had gone biblical in proportion and there were simply fewer people around to make calls, freeing the lines. None of that mattered to the bleeding and anxious man cradling the phone.

"Carol, it's Russ."

There was a pause on the other end of the line before a gravelly voice answered, "I told you to stop calling." His ex sounded as rough as Mike Ditka's mustache, the result of twenty years of unfiltered Camels.

"Hear me out," Russ said. "I'm gonna keep this short and sweet, just like you. I know I did a lot of shitty things over the years—"

"If you need me to bail you out again, you can forget it." This bridge was torched long ago, if not napalmed.

"It's not that. I gotta get this off my chest now or I might not get another chance. I'm sorry about that thing with the landlord's wife, calling the nine-hundred numbers, and your Momma's jewelry. I love you and... and I wanna see you in heaven. I'll keep a spot for you, or vice versa. Kiss the kids for me." Russ paused for a second, confused. Then he flew into a wild rage. "That bitch hung up on me. Un-fucking-believable. I take it all back!"

He shattered his phone on the wall and then sank to the ground while sobbing uncontrollably.

Mike approached him after realizing no one else cared. "It's okay, man, you made your peace with her. That's what's important."

Russ paused his blubbering. "What in the fuck are you brats looking at? Shouldn't you make some calls?"

The guys listened and feverishly dialed their own loved ones to give warnings and say final goodbyes. Charlie eventually reached his parents.

"Stop worrying," his dad said. "You know we're in the boondocks. Plus, the neighbors have set up a watch for suspicious activity and the Johnsons from down the way have their four wheelers and shotguns out. You'd think it was the Fourth of July the way they're carrying on."

"Dad, you gotta be careful. This isn't a joke."

"We'll ride it out till this whole thing blows over."

"It's not gonna blow over, this is for real. We've seen things. We've done things..."

His father sighed. "If so, we're in a good place. I've got a cupboard of dried goods and energy bars and your mom's been canning fruits and veggies for years. We've got a creek for water, and we can always harvest the wildlife. Maybe you should try and get down here? We're not really that far away."

"That's not possible. Jim tried to drive two miles, and I doubt he made it. We might be stuck here for—"

Like Russ's call, the connection dropped.

"Check it out, here come some soldiers," Smokey said, and everyone hurried to the window.

Talk about a letdown.

"They don't have guns," Rob noted and the realization came like a kick to the groin. The soldiers looked to have been through a meat-grinder and were now searching for victims of their own. There would be no rescue.

Russ stopped his sniveling and opened yet another beer. "There's your defense cuts. Fuckin' Democrats."

Chapter 13
The Hard Times
of Marquell Washington

Prisoner 10046, a.k.a. Marquell Washington, peered through his cell door into the darkness as shotgun blasts grew nearer. It looked like the guards wanted space for the new arrivals, and his already short life expectancy shrank to minutes.

Situations like this tend to make one ponder how they ended up behind bars in the first place. In Marquell's case, having a single mom funded by ten-dollar blowjobs and welfare schemes was a good start. Even worse, her powerful crack addiction meant he was on his own since the beginning.

From shoplifting to being an eight-year-old drug mule, Marquell had learned the game on the street and joined the fast track to hard-core thuggery. By his twelfth birthday he'd mastered the art of the sucker punch and even committed his first murder. No one besides his mom's pimp ever realized she was gone, let alone cared.

Far from feeling any self-pity, the dreadlocked and powerfully-built inmate smiled broadly while reminiscing. He'd combined street smarts with an unnatural love of reading developed in juvenile detention, and books like Sun Tzu's *Art of War* had taught him to control the backstreets of Chicago like his own personal fiefdom. The Black Lords, a gang known for their brand of violent street justice, were impressed as Marquell ran his block and rose through their ranks one crime at a time.

He fought, stole, threatened and killed his way to the top, getting tons of money, women and drugs along the way. It was power, however, that Marquell lusted after, and that brought out his sadistic side. Foes that crossed him died painfully, with no quarter given, and no questions asked.

He was a monster, and a talented one at that. So talented that the F.B.I. collared him on federal Rico statutes for racketeering and extortion. They would have had him on eight counts of murder one, but the key witness suffered an unfortunate "accident" involving a chainsaw and a blowtorch. The trial and resulting tabloid circus put the national spotlight on Marquell and made him a star in the underworld. Lockup hadn't been horrible. He ran his gang from inside, settling scores and consolidating power, and still managed to get drugs and even sex from a fat prison counselor when needed.

His major problems came from the Latino inmates and their constant attempts on his life. However, this beef gave Marquell a stage for his craft. First, he strangled Captain Juan Garcia of the United Mexican Mafia and framed the 13th Street Crew. While they fought it out, he poisoned *Gordo* Carlos of *Hermanos Locos* in the cafeteria. Fat Carlos was face down in the mystery meat for less than five minutes before they mistakenly retaliated against the *Chicano Playeros* in the weight room with a handful of shanks and a homemade taser.

Marquell's Black Lords soon filled the power vacuum and the inner city Machiavelli led a massacre. With a stratospheric IQ and no morality to speak of, Marquell was capable of anything. He could've been somebody, given a different upbringing. Now he sat in a squalid ten-by-ten cell awaiting summary execution, all because one of his homeboys dropped a dime to avoid a five-year stretch.

He instantly snapped back into the present as footsteps echoed down the hallway.

Warden McCabe often joked about building the prison inside the ghetto in order to save on gas money. No one ever said he had a sense of humor. What he did have was a powerful drive for money, and like Marquell, a total lack of scruples. Working with the governor and mayor to tear down blighted neighborhoods for the maximum-security prison was a major coup and the project was completed in record time. Of course, several sweetheart deals made in the process didn't hurt.

He already treated the inmates like roaches and after martial law failed, stomping them was the logical choice. With the breakdown of society complete, he was the law, and the soon-to-be empty prison would be his personal domain. Filling it with wealthy tenants was his next step, though he wasn't interested in cash, titles or deeds. Gold would be king, and the helicopters landing in the yard were loaded with suitcases of bullion and uncirculated coins.

For now though, he focused on another vice – revenge. "Have you heard the good news, Mr. Washington? You're scheduled for early release," Warden McCabe said in a friendly manner, his smile far too wide. The fake smile evaporated. "Actually, I wanted to tell you in person that Isaac and Slick Luke are not with us any longer. It seems their accommodations were needed by people that were actually worth a shit."

Marquell was stunned by the news of his lieutenants' deaths but kept his emotions in check. "You're right, those niggas weren't worth a shit."

"Not the sentimental type I see. Nonetheless, you'll be seeing them shortly," the warden said softly, as if speaking to a child. "Your schemes have been a thorn in my side like you wouldn't believe. And staging that riot on Christmas last year, that really was over the top."

"I ain't done scheming yet, bitch."

"Oh but you are. Have you ever owned a pet?" Marquell ignored the question. "No, I don't suppose you would have, being a member of the permanent underclass. I myself had a pet snake growing up. A python, actually. Once a month I'd put a hamster down in its cage. For a while it would keep doing typical hamster things, nibbling on lettuce, wriggling his little nose, totally oblivious to the danger."

"Cool story, bro."

"Eventually, the hamster would see the snake and freeze, you see, his little brain couldn't comprehend the reality staring him in his teeny tiny face. Then he would snap out of his denial and run around in circles, looking for an exit. Of course, he wouldn't find one, and so his next step would be to squeal and squeal and squeal, hoping I'd rescue him."

Marquell turned his back as the warden continued. "Realizing help wasn't coming, he'd frantically dig at the floor. Digging, digging, digging, like he could tunnel out through the glass." He glanced at his shiny Vacheron Constantin, a watch far too expensive for an honest federal employee. "Look at the time. I need to greet some minor celebrities at the helicopter pad. Paying guests, you understand."

The shotgun blasts picked up again in the distance and were even closer this time. Having gloated sufficiently, Warden McCabe began to walk away and then paused for a moment. "Oh, and one more thing. Start digging."

Alone again in the dark, Marquell did indeed go full-hamster as the pressure hit him square on. "I can't go out like this!" he screamed while ripping up his bed, looking for something, anything he could use. For what purpose, he had no clue.

He pounded on the cell door with all his might, but it didn't budge. So Marquell turned, and, in an astonishing feat of strength, ripped the metal toilet from the floor. It too clanged off the door uselessly as cold water pooled around him.

Marquell could hear Steve, the prison's most demented guard, taunting his victims while reloading, "Don't worry, dirtballs, I got enough for everyone."

Footsteps approached once again and Marquell's broad shoulders slumped. Lights out.

Only it wasn't Steve.

An angelic voice whispered to him from the shadows. "I'm springing you, baby." It was Susan, his counselor and pseudo-love interest.

The cell door clanked open and Marquell cautiously stepped into the hallway as Susan threw her arms around his muscular frame. "You know I wouldn't leave you."

Marquell smirked as he realized all his planning, tactics and ruthlessness hadn't mattered one bit. In the end, it was his love of fat women that saved the day. "Let me hold that flashlight, in case we run into trouble."

She handed it over and he gripped the Maglite tightly. The weight and smoothness felt oddly comforting in his hands. "There's one more thing, what's the cell block code?"

Susan realized for the first time that Marquell might not be the sweet-talking cuddle-bunny of her dreams. She ignored the chill creeping down her spine. "I don't know it and—" Susan's words were cut short as the Maglite crashed heavily into her jaw. The impact turned the flashlight on, and a stream of teeth and blood glittered momentarily in the beam before falling out of sight.

He yanked Susan from the floor by her hair. "What's the fucking code?"

She sputtered it out between sobs, and Marquell dumped her to the ground like a piece of garbage. Things were about to get interesting for prisoner 10046.

Chapter 14
Clown-Car Cluster-Fuck

Blake's hands trembled as he opened the back door to his fiancée's apartment, his optimism already robbed by the discovery of a shattered balcony window. They quickly fanned out and found signs of a raucous bachelorette party, but no girls.

"Guys, come out here," Cliff said ominously from the living room. There was a large, dark red puddle in the middle of the carpet. Blood red.

Jim sank to his knees. "Oh no. No, no, no."

Blake stuck a finger into the liquid, sniffed it, and then put it to his lips. "Relax, it's red wine."

"Quick, grab some seltzer water," Cliff said, cutting the tension down noticeably. "The girls must have left."

They were so relieved in fact, that nobody saw the G-string wearing man coming down the stairwell behind them, and the muscle-bound stripper pounced on Cliff in an instant.

"What the hell?" the banker said as the weight landed squarely on his back.

Blake raised his weapon to fire.

Click.

To nobody's surprise, the shady-looking gun Smokey had purchased for a twenty-sack of weed and a cracked water bong failed miserably.

Cliff tried to fling the bigger man off him while Blake grabbed a nearby barstool and bashed at the spray-tanned assailant, accomplishing little as the slippery man ignored the blows and focused on his squirming prey.

Jim put his gun to the back of the stripper's head and pulled the trigger. The exit wound spewed Blake with gore and the spent bullet struck him squarely in the chest, knocking him down.

"I'm hit," he said while instinctively reaching for the injury. But the bullet had slowed just enough, and there wasn't one.

"Thank God." Jim lifted his friend up and turned to a visibly shaken Cliff. "You okay?"

"Good thing I had my coat on. Men's Warehouse. Fuck yeah I like how I look," he said with a nervous laugh.

Blake pointed to the body. "And what was this asshole doing here?"

"I can give you two guesses, but you'll only need one," Cliff answered.

"Pretty cocky for a guy that just got tea-bagged a minute ago," Blake said. "Anyways, don't tell the guys about the stripper. We'll never hear the end of it."

Jim shook his head. "My wife and your fiancée are nowhere to be found, and that's what you're worried about?"

There was a loud crashing noise downstairs as a crowd ran through the front door at full speed. The gunshot had gained unwanted attention and the mob began storming one apartment after another.

Cliff threw his hands up in the air. "Really?"

Blake took the lead. "Grab whatever we can and let's go out the back." They ransacked the fridge and rustled up a dozen frozen dinners, some bottled water and a half-eaten penis-shaped cake.

"This is it?" Cliff asked.

"Jen doesn't cook, and this is Chicago. You know there's a restaurant on every block." Blake searched for something in the back of the fridge. "Where the hell is it?" he mumbled under his breath.

Cliff peeked around his shoulder. "Do you need help finding something?"

"It's nothing," Blake said and then followed the others outside. Now all they had to do was make it to the car and navigate past about a thousand bloodthirsty savages. Piece of cake. Piece of penis cake.

*   *   *

"Give it a rest. You're not coming in," Charlie said out the window. The men had shoved a couch between the door and the stairwell, but it still threatened to cave in at any moment as more cannibals crowded onto the porch.

"We need to clear a path for Jim and the others," Trent said. "It's looking like the welfare office at the first of the month out there."

"Do you think you can shoot a few?" Bruce said. "Thin the herd out so to speak."

"I don't have many bullets left, but sure, why not?"

Charlie frowned. "You might attract more."

"Here comes Cliff's car," Trent said as his eyes widened. "And they're coming in hot too."

This was an understatement as the Lexus had four flat tires, two busted windows and three infected madmen clinging to the top, covered-wagon style. Several hundred more trailed behind on foot.

"Looks like we've got ourselves a real clown-car cluster-fuck here," Russ said, his speech slurred and his scalp bleeding profusely. "I'm sitting this one out."

"Trent, you're up," Mike said.

The cop hung out the window, careful not to go as far as Russ had, and blasted away at the shambling creatures. Just then, the car rolled up with sparks jumping and road kill flying. It didn't stop.

The whole apartment groaned as the car slammed into the porch with a crash and tipped it over. Debris and dead bodies landed on the luxury vehicle as it was literally raining men.

Charlie formed a hasty plan. "We've got an extension ladder on the roof we can drop down. Rob, let's go."

The two raced upstairs while Trent fired randomly, taking down a bearded man in a hospital gown and a school crossing guard. Jim and the others made their way from the wreckage but had nowhere to go.

Charlie whistled as they lowered the heavy ladder into the alleyway.

Jim and Blake came up in no time, but Cliff seemed to have lost a step. He finally made it to the top and then collapsed as Rob yanked the ladder up. Moments later, they gathered in the living room.

"Any sign of the girls?" Mike asked. Jim shook his head, and Mike continued. "Russ took a beating. How did you guys do?

"We're in one piece, but as you can tell," Blake said and pointed to the gray matter dripping from his clothing, "it wasn't pretty."

Russ hugged him. "I always said my nephew had brains. Now it's official."

"Real funny." Blake caught a whiff of beer on his uncle's breath and noticed the extra cans lying about. "Are you guys fucking drunk?"

"Maybe, what's it to you?" Russ answered. "You aren't my probation officer last I checked."

"We could've been dead for all you knew, and you're over here getting liquored up. Shit, we haven't even been gone an hour."

Russ pointed at the wreckage. "It looks like Cliff was drinking too."

Charlie nodded. "He did take care of our porch problem, but what happened?"

"I had tunnel vision or something. I think from all the pressure..." Cliff's face darkened. "You know, it would've gone smoother if some of you pansies hadn't stayed behind."

Bruce realized the frat brothers seriously outnumbered them and tried to calm his friend. "Take a breather, you did good. Everybody's on edge." He pointed at Blake's garbage bag. "What's that?"

"We grabbed some food." Blake turned to Mike. "And we got a special surprise for you." He expected to hear some laughs while pulling the smashed cake out of the bag.

"I guess we need to have a long chat," Mike said with a wry smile.

As Mike caught them up on the news, Cliff retreated to the bathroom to check on his throbbing arm. He took his jacket off and found two small bruises near his shoulder. The skin felt warm to the touch, and brown pus shot out when he nudged the spot. Someone knocked on the door.

Cliff rifled through the medicine cabinet and pulled out a bottle of hydrogen peroxide. He soaked a towel in the solution and wrapped it around his shaking arm like a tourniquet. That's when the labor-like pains hit. His vision blurred and the banker ran to the toilet while blood oozed down his leg.

The knocking continued while someone talked through the door, but Cliff no longer knew what words were, much less what they meant. So he simply stared at the door and waited. Hungrily.

Chapter 15
The Scientific Method

"Open up Cliff, I gotta drop a deuce," Left-Nut said and knocked on the bathroom door. "Seriously, I've got a turtle-head creeping here." There was still no response. "Okay I warned you. I'm coming in."

Cliff surged through the opened door and blasted Left-Nut right out of his sandals. Pinned down like a lamb for the slaughter, Left-Nut somehow grasped Cliff's throat and kept the snapping mouth at bay. Still, a life of swearing and masturbation flashed before his eyes, and there was little to be proud about.

The others thought the two were simply goofing around, but as Left-Nut screamed like a little girl, they saw otherwise. Big Rob dove onto Cliff's back and sunk in a tight chokehold. He carefully pressed underneath Cliff's jaw to avoid getting bitten, and held the much smaller man down while Left-Nut scurried away.

Bruce grabbed a plunger from the bathroom and shoved it in front of his friend's chomping mouth. Cliff promptly crunched into the wood and shattered his front teeth into Tic-Tacs while the others jumped into the struggle with fists, feet, duct tape and Trent's handcuffs.

The cop put his pistol to the struggling man's head as the cuffs carved deeply into Cliff's fleshy wrists. Blake angrily batted the gun away. "That's Cliff. You can't just shoot him."

"Watch me." Trent readied to fire once more.

"Bring him to the roof," Mike said, taking charge of the chaotic situation. Despite Trent's objections, they carried the squirming man out and firmly fastened him to an antenna overlooking the street. Strange as it was, his day was only going to get worse as the group smoked cigarettes and nervously pondered their next step.

"Somebody pull his pants up at least," Blake said.

Left-Nut shook his head. "No thanks. He's got bloody shit all over his legs and besides, he tried to eat me."

"Fine." Blake did the dirty deed himself and gagged as he caught a whiff of the noxious odor.

"It's pretty obvious what we're dealing with here," Russ said and paused to take a long drag. He exhaled. "God-damned zombies."

Charlie threw his hands up. "Have another beer."

"What would you call them, Chuck? They are eating people. If it looks like a zombie and quacks like a zombie, it's a zombie."

Smokey disagreed. "No, they don't seem to be undead. You know, like vampires or ghouls and the like." He put his arm around Cliff and ruffled his hair. "Take our friend here. He didn't go after Left-Nut's brains for starters, which would have been a typical zombie response. And secondly, Russ, how do zombies always die in movies?"

"You shoot 'em in the head. Blow their brains out."

"And we've seen they can be killed like normal people, so that means—"

"You dumbasses might as well be arguing about how many angels fit on the head of a pin," Trent said. "Blah, blah, blah. It doesn't matter what you call them. All I know is, this one's about to learn a valuable lesson about the circle of life."

"Oh give it a rest, tough guy." Mike stepped between Trent and his target once more. "We need to study Cliff to see what he's capable of. Then we'll know how to deal with these... these things."

"Zombies," Russ added with emphasis.

"Maybe they can starve or get diseases," Mike said. "Hell, they might all freeze to death in the winter for all we know. Cliff can be our guinea pig."

Trent still wasn't convinced. "What, you think you're the Jane Goodall of zombies or something?"

"This might be the difference between life and death for us," Mike said firmly.

"It does makes sense," Charlie added. Everyone with the exception of Left-Nut and Trent agreed, so Cliff, or what was left of him, would continue to exist for now.

"Back to the movies," Russ said. "Every time a zombie gets spared, like this one right here, it always ends up killing someone when they least expect it."

"Get to the point," Blake said.

"In this scenario, as I intend to be drunk all the time, and I'm pretty fucked up right now, I'd guess it's gonna be me. So, if we're not gonna kill it, can we at least make it less dangerous? Kind of give me a sporting chance."

"I'm on it," Trent said nonchalantly and wandered back inside, emerging minutes later with rubber gloves, a cordless drill and a pair of rusty needle nose pliers. The macabre day got even more so as he ripped the duct tape from Cliff's mouth while the blistering sun beat down and the ice cream song played in the background.

"I've got good news and bad news," Trent said. "The good news is there's no co-pay. The bad news is there's no painkiller. Say ah."

The cop chuckled at his own clichéd joke and jabbed the whirring drill into Cliff's mouth. A wet, crackling noise arose as blood and bits of tooth whizzed about, flung by the rotation of the drill. Trent fished around with the pliers and plucked out several mangled teeth, dropping them one at a time into a beer can.

"You really are a sadistic son of a bitch," Blake said and clinched his fists.

"I wanted to put him out of his misery, remember?"

Russ walked over. "I don't think he's feeling anything, see?" He put his cigarette out on Cliff's face, and the tied up man didn't even blink.

Left-Nut kicked Cliff in the groin, just to be sure. He didn't flinch.

"See? We already learned something important," Mike said. "They don't feel pain."

"We also know Zombie Cliff won't be having kids," Left-Nut said.

Blake gave Left-Nut a "shut the fuck up" look, and he did. Russ and Trent, however, continued to torment Cliff and started tossing empty beer cans at his head.

Meanwhile, Bruce decided to suck up to the others since he was now the odd man out. He needed to do it quickly, though, as they appeared to be heading for a real *Lord of the Flies* scenario. "Rob, that was some chokehold you used there. You'll have to show it to me sometime."

"Sure," Rob said, proceeding to choke him unconscious before he even had time to protest. Bruce's limp body crumpled to a heap on the ground.

"I don't think that's what he meant," Charlie said and slapped Bruce awake.

This idiocy was the last straw for Blake. "I'm going in." He looked at Cliff. "Sorry, buddy, you deserved better." Then, glaring at the others he added, "You assholes will regret this when you sober up."

Russ shrugged. "Who said anything about sobering up?"

Chapter 16
Rules, Regulations
and Rejects

The sun sank below the horizon and the gang's drunken bravado went with it. As darkness crept in and the wails of the dying rang across the city, the friends gathered like scared boy scouts crowded around a campfire. Only the monsters lurking in the shadows were real, and they were hungry. So the men focused on what they could control, which, as it turned out, wasn't much.

"The way I see it, we need to set ground rules if we're gonna survive till help comes," Mike said while surveying Charlie's trashed living room. The triple whammy of body odor, desperation and Cliff's diarrhea lingered like an unwelcome guest.

"What help?" Bruce said. "We're toast and you know it."

"Regardless, Mike's right," Charlie said. "What do you have in mind?"

"For starters, we need to have a food czar so that—"

"Hold on a minute there, Fidel." Russ's face darkened. "I didn't spend a year knee-deep in muddy rice paddies and slant-eyes so that—"

Blake rose to his feet. "Dammit, you weren't in Vietnam! You were like ten years old, you fuckin' liar. Shut up for once and let Mike speak."

"Czar just means boss. Let's just say we need a food boss, okay?" Russ nodded and Mike continued. "I nominate myself because, well, you guys are all dumbasses compared to me. Anyone disagree?" Nobody did. "Good. I did a quick inventory of the fridge here and the one upstairs, and it isn't good. We'll need to start rationing. Like yesterday."

"I could use a bite to eat, now that you've mentioned it. What've we got?" Rob asked, his stomach grumbling.

"Stale ramen noodles, ketchup, mustard, two boxes of cereal, and the food you guys snagged from Jen's place."

"That's it?" Bruce said. "Seriously, does Gandhi do your grocery shopping? Rob's probably got more food stuck between his teeth."

"Why cook when I can pay a wetback five bucks for a greasy sack of meat and cheese?" Trent asked. "And I know it'll be damn tasty too."

Mike shook his head. "Pissing on sleeping bums and trading speeding tickets for dates is fine, but cooking's beneath you?"

"Sorry, but cereal's all I had," Smokey added and gazed at his feet. "Charlie and I always order Thai food or pizza." He conveniently left out the sizeable stash of stoner food and pot tucked behind a velvet portrait of Al Pacino in his living room. That, he would save for a rainy day.

"I think it's time for fatty to go on a diet," Bruce said, still ablaze over the choking incident. "I bet he could go two weeks without food and still be a total lard-ass."

"Maybe I'll eat your share, you little shit," Rob replied, showing an uncharacteristic flash of anger. Food was the one thing he took seriously.

"Everybody gets the same share, and I'll be making the portions," Mike said, trying to defuse the situation before Bruce got stomped. "With the eight of us eating almost nothing, we have about three days of food."

Russ arched an eyebrow. "I think the real question is how much booze do we have?"

"A ton, but I wouldn't drink it. Alcohol dehydrates you, and who knows how long the water will keep coming out of the tap. Then we'll have to catch rainwater."

"You might as well tell a fish not to swim," Blake said, and his uncle nodded in agreement. At least the man knew his limitations.

"We can fill the bottles and the bathtub with water, and the kiddie pool too," Jim said.

"That's a great idea," Mike said. "Now that we have food and water covered, we should talk about ways to prevent another Cliff-type situation."

"When Vidu got bit, he changed quickly, same as Mrs. Stone downstairs," Charlie said.

Mike pursed his lips. "Cliff definitely had bite marks on his arm, but it barely broke the skin. That might be why it took him so long to turn."

"And Vidu was ripped to shreds," Charlie said.

"It seems the worse the bite, the quicker the infection spreads. Must be the saliva or even bacteria in the mouth. It could be in the blood for all we know," Mike said, thinking out loud.

"Sounds like turbo-rabies or Super-AIDS or something," Left-Nut said.

"No, Super-AIDS is what you caught last night," Charlie quipped. "But seriously, I don't know what's crazier, the zombie apocalypse or the fact you banged a crippled girl. I bet you're literally the biggest scumbag left on the planet."

Left-Nut shrugged. "Judge me however you want, I could care less. A piece of ass is a piece of ass. But remind me, who gave you that black eye again? Oh yeah, you got pimp-slapped...by a pimp. Real classy."

Mike cleared his throat. "We can all agree Left-Nut's a creeper, and yes, Charlie had sex with a hooker last night, but let's stay on topic. We need a protocol to check for bites after anyone leaves the apartment. Something we do every single time."

"Leave the apartment? You first," Bruce said.

"The reality is that we're gonna have to get food soon, or else..." Mike's words trailed off.

"So what do you have in mind? Like, a quarantine or something?" Charlie said. "I'll tell you right now, I'm not getting tied up. I saw what happened to Cliff."

"I was thinking more along the lines of a strip search, you know, just a quick check for bites."

Trent faked a laugh. "The gay-wad wants us all to get naked, imagine that. Undressing me with your eyes not enough anymore, Liberace?"

But the others agreed to the plan, and it was settled. Anyone returning to the apartment would get checked without exception. What happened to those bitten was still up for grabs, but a chilling precedent had been made.

The guys got to work and Jim filled beer bottles with water while Russ emptied them of beer. Meanwhile, Rob and Charlie hung black bed sheets over the windows to hide their homemade electricity. People no longer manned the power stations, and it was only a matter of time before a rolling blackout made the dingy three-flat the hottest property in town.

Minutes later, the busy work stopped as the sounds of breaking glass and screams came from the kitchen. Charlie ran in to see Blake convulsing on the floor while Left-Nut cowered underneath the table. Charlie pressed Blake's head down while he frothed and squirmed.

"I guess we should have done that strip-search after all," Trent said while un-holstering his pistol. "I promise he won't feel a thing."

"Put that down before you hurt somebody," Mike said while pulling a shiny silver chain out of Blake's pocket. He examined it and breathed a huge sigh of relief. "Blake's not infected. He's diabetic."

Chapter 17
The Eagle Flies at Midnight

The massive Boeing 747-200B series aircraft cut through the cloudless night sky as it had countless times before. However, the view thirty thousand feet below *Air Force One* was unlike any since the birth of electricity. Darkness dominated the landscape for hundreds of miles in every direction as massive blackouts rolled across the Midwest.

The only light came from the out of control fires now consuming cities and towns, block by block, house by house. Some had been started to contain the infected while others emanated from ruptured gas mains, crashed vehicles, downed power lines and dropped cigarettes.

The mayhem below led to some other firsts in American history. To begin with, Senator Sanders, the President pro tempore of the Senate, had recently taken the oath of office. Such an odd chain of succession came after *Marine One* crashed into the Potomac, the vice president died from a massive heart attack, and the Speaker of the House was eaten on the steps of the Capital Building. The brand new president quickly found himself managing over the fate of the entire world.

A deeply religious man despite occasional sins of the flesh, Thaddeous Willard Sanders believed God had put him in charge at this crucial time for a purpose. Accompanying him was a small group of advisors, family, surviving members of Congress and several reporters. Their destination was an underground base outside Honolulu, the new capital of the withering United States Government and possibly the last safe spot on earth.

Air Force One and its C-5 Galaxy escort had tried to land several times, only to cancel at the last minute. It was simply too risky to jeopardize the mission, even for the sake of family members. Those left on the tarmacs would meet the same fate as their countrymen one bite at a time.

As a testament to the effectiveness of the man-made virus, the top brass had been stunned at how quickly the crisis spiraled out of control. It had jumped from the cities to the suburbs and countryside in a matter of days. The entire continental U.S. showed signs of the novel pathogen within a week, with the only stopgap being the newly constructed and now heavily fortified border wall with Mexico. Ironically, it was the wall built to keep Mexicans out that now effectively kept Americans in.

The military suddenly found itself the last arm of the government still functioning. After charging mobs overran several flat-footed bases, free-fire zones had been set up and some semblance of order returned. The downside was that civilians fleeing the carnage soon had no place to go. It was a necessary evil, one of many to come.

The POTUS slammed a can of Red Bull bearing the presidential seal, then barked orders around his situation table. He hadn't slept in two days, and the strain of presiding over the greatest disaster in history was starting to take its toll. Still, the man furiously scribbled down different scenarios and options as fast as his pen would move. But every plan became irrelevant due to rapidly developing events on the ground. President Sanders wasn't sure who was responsible, but he knew someone would pay dearly.

Stromm Aikens, former war hero, Navy Admiral and current secretary of defense, addressed his boss. "Incurable diseases don't simply show up out of the blue in five major cities on the same day. It's time to counter-punch."

The president nodded in agreement. "Of course. Now who the hell did it?"

"Our last report came from a lab in Idaho that studies wasting diseases and prions. They believe we're dealing with a man-made bug, and an impressive one at that. It seems the pathogen kills off most of the brain but leaves the area responsible for instincts intact. The result is a feral human of sorts, immune to pain but lacking rational thinking skills. Dumb, but deadly."

The president took a deep breath. "Al-Qaeda doesn't have that type of technical knowhow, so we can rule them out right now."

"That's correct, a complex operation like this is definitely nation-state sponsored. The little guys wouldn't be able to pull it off, considering Al-Qaeda couldn't even get their hands on anthrax. That narrows the capable nations down to Russia, Japan, China, India, Israel and Great Britain. Obviously, from that group, the only countries that stand to gain are Russia and China and—"

"It's China. The bastards have wanted to take us down since their famine started, and I'm not sure why we didn't see it coming." The president's last biting comment was meant for Sam Childers, current secretary of state. The silver-tongued former congressman had been engaging China in diplomatic back channels for months, claiming all the while to be making progress.

Mr. Childers rose from his seat. "With all due respect, I don't believe it's the Chinese. They know we couldn't send food aid due to sanctions over the currency spat, and they appreciate us staying out of the Taiwan situation. With rising ethanol output, rampant market speculation and a global decrease in grain production due to an extremely powerful *El Niño* effect—"

"El Niño? Are you serious? The bottom line is they've been eating grass for two years and—"

"There's no *casus belli*, and we have absolutely no record of China possessing advanced bio-weapons. Even if they did, it would be ludicrous to utilize them because we didn't send wheat shipments during a seasonal famine."

The president fixed the secretary of state with a cold and deep stare. "You know what's ludicrous to me? I've seen people walking around after they've been shot four or five times. I saw my secretary claw her child's face off and eat it. If you ask me, this whole damn world has gone ludicrous. Oh, and one more thing, Childers — interrupt me one more time and I will knock your teeth out."

"Sir, we have General Saxby calling in from NORADD," an assistant said and handed over the phone.

"What's the situation in Russia?" the president said.

"Not good," a gravelly voice answered. "They're suffering much the same as us. I've had a direct line to my counterpart for the past forty-five minutes and he's begging for assistance. They've declared martial law and are trying to stop the spread any way they can. They're even bombing their own cities. Novgorod and St. Petersburg have been completely wiped off of the map."

The president took a deep breath. "And NATO?"

"They've grounded all commercial flights and have a quarantine line in the Crimean Mountains. It's holding for now. Great Britain's navy has set up a ten-mile kill zone around their territorial waters. It's every man for himself."

The president's face grew redder by the second. "What about our satellite imagery on China? Is there anything peculiar going on?"

"We haven't noticed anything out of the ordinary. No blackouts, no fires, no explosions."

"Everything's golden there?"

"It appears that way," the general said.

"It's common sense that if Russia is infected and China isn't..." Secretary Aikens let his words trail off.

"One moment, Mr. President." The general put the phone down while a message was relayed and returned a minute later. "I have some bad news. The Green Zone in Baghdad has fallen. Kabul seems to have been overrun as well."

"What happened?"

"The Iranians are making a play for the Mideast. They've stirred up trouble with the Mahdi army in Iraq and have sent in several hundred suicide bombers. They've also sent waves of single engine kamikazes and Silkworm missiles at our carrier strike group near the Straits of Hormuz. We've lost a carrier and another is heavily damaged."

"My God. A capital ship is a red line."

"There's more. Hezbollah is raining rockets into Israel by the hundreds, and a massive dirty bomb has exploded in Tel Aviv."

The president's eyes turned to steel as he snapped out orders. "I want a full evacuation of our troops from the Middle East, Dunkirk style. I don't care if it's ugly, just get them out. Steal cruise ships, fishing boats, do whatever. Any of our people not out to sea in twelve hours is dead. I also want a strike group headed to the Pacific. Get Major Thomas in here with the pigskin."

The serious-looking aide in charge of carrying the president's emergency satchel entered the room with what was commonly referred to as the nuclear football. The aide opened up the black bag and revealed a thick briefcase with a numbered lock. After dialing up the code, the case was opened to reveal a laptop computer, a black notepad and several folders.

"Get me the info on China," the president said.

"Sir, that's the folder labeled Red Dragon."

The President opened the folder and read the code aloud as the aide typed. "Access code seven-two-Romeo-India-Papa-four-Sierra-Oscar-Bravo-six-niner."

"What setting, Mr. President?"

"Setting?"

"It's how many nukes we send. Think of it like cooking a steak, sir."

"Set it to well done. I don't want a blade of grass over there for a century." The only thing left to do was hit "enter" on the small keyboard.

"I think you should be the one to finish this." The major turned around, unable to witness the final keystroke.

"Of course." President Sanders reached forward.

The secretary of state trembled at such a blatant power grab. "You need the approval of Congress before using nuclear weapons, and we haven't even declared war. What if China isn't behind this?"

"If you hadn't noticed, half of Congress ate the other half."

"We're dealing with complex constitutional issues here. You weren't even elected and the legal authority to—"

President Sanders tapped the computer. "I have all the authority I need right here."

"But they'll retaliate and hit our major cities. We still have hope of curing the infection and retaking the nation. We can rebuild. We can start over."

"Hit our cities? Don't you mean graveyards? This is the only option we have left. It's now our duty to punish the aggressors, even if it's the last act of our nation." A pale, fanatical gleam had taken shape in the president's eyes. He was now sure of his path to salvation.

"You'll be seen as the biggest war criminal in history, right up there with Hitler and Stalin."

"You don't get it, Childers. After today, there is no history."

The discussion was over. One congressman was unable to deal with the enormity of the situation and ran to the bathroom to vomit. More people were about to be killed in the next few hours than in all the wars of history.

President Sanders reached for the keyboard and paused as his officials gathered around him. What he was about to say would either echo through the ages or disappear with the human race.

"The godless heathen, Friedrich Nietzsche, stated that hope is the worst of evils, for it prolongs the torments of man." The witnesses put their heads down and several sobbed loudly. "We are now devoid of hope, yet we continue to suffer. We take solitude in God's plan and understand we are mere instruments of his will. Let us break the seventh seal, punish those that have transgressed upon our Nation and the Lord, and bask in his righteous vengeance."

He struck the key and hundreds of intercontinental ballistic missiles launched from silos and submarines around the world. Traveling at fifteen thousand miles per hour, they'd quickly reach their destinations in the Far East.

The plane was silent for the next five minutes. Finally, President Sanders picked up the phone. "Saxby, have they retaliated yet?"

"No, and they must have already detected our birds. It's quite strange." There was a loud commotion in the control room and the pandemonium was clear over the phone. "This isn't good. They're knocking out our satellites. We'll be blind without them."

The president rubbed his temples and looked around the room. "How come we didn't know they had this capability?"

Secretary of Defense Aikens put his hands on the president's shoulders. "Sir, the C.I.A. doesn't know their assholes from their elbows. We didn't know the Soviet Union was collapsing until it was on CNN."

"There's no use in finger pointing now since everyone who screwed up is dead," the president said. "But we have to act. What do you recommend, Strom?"

Secretary Aikens took a deep breath. "I believe this calls for Operation Omega. It puts the scorched into scorched earth. We'll launch everything while we can. Iraq, Iran... Saudi Arabia, everything over there. The Chinese can use the oil in five thousand years when it stops glowing."

The president shuffled through the folders and stopped at the biggest and most dangerous-looking one. "You're sure about this?"

"In a few minutes our capabilities are going to be taken back to the 1960's. It's now or never."

The president rubbed sweat from his brow and opened the ominous black folder labeled with an omega symbol. He read the code aloud while typing. "Access code four-three-Alpha-Tango-Oscar-two-seven-Yankee-Zulu-Tango. Set it to well done."

The secretary of state realized this was his only chance to stop the unfolding madness. Smashing the laptop could save millions of lives, maybe the world itself. He inched forward and balled his hand into a fist, hoping to break the screen with a solid punch.

One of the marines assigned to watch the secretary's every move, however, had noticed the man's ashen appearance. Before Childers could act, he found himself in a powerful headlock. Two other marines struggled to drag him out of the room, brutally dislocating his shoulder in the process.

The president got right in his face. "What the hell are you doing? You know that—"

Secretary Childers screamed through the pain, "For god sakes, our men are down there! This is genocide, you crazy son of a—"

The stiff jab from the president shut Childers up. "I told you not to interrupt me." It was a well-placed sucker punch that knocked the secretary of state's dentures right out of his mouth. They skittered across the floor and disappeared under a chair.

Secretary Aikens ignored the melee. "We need to find out why they haven't launched their nukes. If they wait much longer, we'll knock out their capability of striking back completely. It doesn't make sense. There's no rope-a-dope when it comes to nuclear exchanges."

As Childers kicked and screamed, the president steadied himself and launched the next round of missiles, this time with no speech and a swollen right hand.

Another aide rushed into the room. "Mr. President." All eyes turned to the young airman. "We have word from the Pacific Fleet. Their radar has picked up a large naval force leaving China."

"How large?" Secretary Aikens said.

"It's the biggest ever."

The secretary of defense nodded grimly. "There's our answer it seems. China doesn't want to destroy us, it wants to own us."

The plot had been as elegant as it was insidious. China had been crippled by a currency war and then ravaged by a massive drought, and the world had shrugged while millions died. So, rather than fight Mother Nature, they used her to their advantage. The man-made virus would depopulate North America and the Chinese would use the open land to start over, much like the pilgrims had done hundreds of years earlier. Only small-pox had nothing on the Chinese virus.

The new revelation strengthened the president's resolve. "Turn this plane south, our plans have changed." He looked to Secretary Aikens. "Tell President Goya we're annexing Northern Mexico, and it's not up for discussion."

Chapter 18
Operation Ben-Gay

Russ lit a cowboy killer and cracked a hesitant smile. "Blake's not turning into a zombie?"

"Not according to his symptoms and the information on his medical bracelet. This is a diabetic attack," Mike said.

Rob smiled and dabbed a wet cloth to Blake's clammy forehead. "Diabetes, that's not so bad. Right?"

"It's a death sentence unless we can find some insulin," Mike said and swiveled his head around the room. "Did anyone know about this?"

"He never mentioned it to me," Jim said.

"Blake's been taking a lot of personal days, but he said it was for wedding stuff," Bruce added, clearly shaken up.

"Why would he hide it?" Smokey said.

Trent holstered his gun. "Probably the same reason Mike hid the fact that he chugs cock. It's embarrassing."

Mike's eyes burned. "First off, it's not embarrassing to have a disease or to be gay. Second off, I never actually acted on my urges."

"You're a virgin?" the cop said in his typical schoolyard bully fashion.

"No, I've slept with lots of chicks."

"That doesn't count and you know it." Trent sensed blood in the water. "We've got ourselves a thirty-year old virgin here."

"Yeah, what a loser," Left-Nut said, always one to bring himself up by putting others down.

"I'm not dignifying that with a response, but I do have one question, Trent. Why are you so eager to shoot people?

I know Cliff was an asshole, but Blake's been your friend for years and you didn't even hesitate."

"I'm not taking any chances. I'll shoot you in the face if you get bit, and I don't care if you're the Pope, my mom or a bum off the street."

"What do we do?" Bruce asked. "We can't exactly march down to the drugstore and fill out a prescription."

"We can check Mrs. Stone's apartment downstairs," Charlie said. "I know she gets medicine delivered because the dumbshit mailman keeps putting it in my mailbox."

"Do you know what it was?" Mike said.

"Fuck if I know, but it's worth finding out. Plus, she might have food."

"That's not a half bad idea, Chuck, but who's got the balls to go?" Russ said. "I mean, I will because he's family, but who's coming with me?"

Fat, drunk and bloody, Russ wasn't the type of man you wanted to follow in line at the gas station, much less into a situation where you might get eaten alive. Every fiber of Charlie's body screamed to sit this one out, to let someone else volunteer, but he'd already seen one friend die and wasn't prepared to see another.

"I'm in," he said numbly, feeling like the words left someone else's mouth.

"Count me out," Trent said predictably.

"Ditto," Left-Nut added.

None of the others volunteered, and Russ flew into a mini-rage. "Look, this isn't D-Day. We're just going right downstairs, so stop being a bunch of faggots." He glanced at Mike. "Sorry, homosexuals."

Mike blinked rapidly a few times in exasperation before composing himself. "He's right. We need to start acting like a team if we want to survive. And since I'm in charge of the food, if you don't help, you don't eat."

They bickered over the details for a while until coming up with what they considered a somewhat decent plan. An hour later, the men gathered on the roof, partially sobered up and ready to rock.

Cliff had continued to glare at everyone, until it got creepy to the point where Smokey had to blindfold him with an old sock. This seemed to make the stockbroker even more desperate, and now he sniffed the air like a bloodhound.

"That pissed him off," Trent said while walking with Smokey to the front of the building.

"He'd be even more mad if he knew what I use that sock for in my spare time."

Trent chuckled as the pair readied their diversion. Meanwhile, Big Rob raised the ladder into position over a back alleyway dimly lit by a handful of burning cars. Below, a host of creatures milled about in the haze, casting large, ominous shadows. They went berserk as Trent cranked up hardcore gangster rap on his boom box and Smokey shot a roman candle right into their ranks.

The cop banged on pots and pans for effect. "Hey, you morons, up here!"

While every zombie within a quarter mile swarmed the front side of the house, Rob dropped the ladder out back and nodded to his waiting friends. It was time.

Charlie had seen more action in the past ten hours than he had in the past ten years of his life, and had the cuts, bruises and sexually transmitted diseases to prove it. And so he hesitated for a moment.

"Move it, Nancy," Russ said. Charlie obliged and soon found himself on the ground, scanning the alley for any stragglers. Seeing none, he signaled for Russ and Left-Nut to come down and then pushed in a window screen. They climbed inside and were, for the time being, out of sight.

"Yuck, this place smells like old lady," Left-Nut said as he rummaged through the cabinets.

Russ smirked. "You think this is bad, wait till the corpses in the street start rotting. Hell, when I was in Vietnam..."

Charlie ignored Russ and focused on raiding the wooden medicine cabinet next to the fridge. He found blood pressure medicine, hemorrhoid ointment and some pills he'd never heard of. It all went into the sack.

"Did she have any good prescriptions? Oxy or codeine or something?" Left-Nut asked and was ignored.

Charlie moved on to the fridge and spied a plastic baggie in the vegetable drawer. "But look what we have here." He pulled out several vials of clear liquid as a look of pride crossed his face. "Insulin."

Left-Nut peered past Charlie and groaned. "She doesn't have anything to eat in the fridge either? It's like food is illegal in this damned apartment."

Russ opened a pantry door and revealed row upon row of canned goods tucked away inside. His face turned sour as he took a closer look. "It's all cat food. Every stinkin' can."

"Where's the cat?" Left-Nut asked.

Charlie grimaced. "She didn't have one."

"Oh that's gross," Left-Nut said, a little too loudly.

"Lower your damn voice," Charlie said. "And I wouldn't get too judgmental. It's our dinner."

Russ pointed to the bonanza of potted meat. "That stuff is dangerous. Too fatty."

The schoolteacher looked at Russ's ample gut. "I think that ship has sailed." They tossed the cans into trash bags and then looked for anything else that might be useful.

Left-Nut zeroed in on a picture of a youthful looking Mrs. Stone on her nightstand. "She used to be pretty friggin' hot back in the day. I'd totally hit it. Kinda sad Rob smashed her like a wet turd, ya know?"

"She was pretty," Charlie admitted and rubbed the fist-sized knot on the back of his head. "And judging from these other pictures in here, she was a bird watcher too."

Left-Nut looked at Charlie sideways. "Who gives a shit?"

"It means there's probably a pair of binoculars in here we can grab. Which would come in mighty handy."

They continued rifling around as the racket from outside covered their tracks, and Russ found something of interest in a dresser drawer. But it wasn't a pair of binoculars. In fact, it was far from it. He threw the giant, pink, spiked vibrator to the floor and dry heaved while the others tried to hold in their laughter.

"Mrs. Stone was a dirty girl," Left-Nut said approvingly. "I like it."

"Keep looking, those binoculars have to be close by," Charlie said, hoping to erase the pink monstrosity from his mind by focusing on the task at hand.

Left-Nut popped open a small cylindrical device he found in a leather case. Mrs. Stone's last boyfriend had left the electric voice box there before dying the previous winter while shoveling snow. She had kept it around for other purposes.

The discovery should not have been a big deal, but Left-Nut couldn't control himself. He held it to his throat and created a loud robotic voice. "Bow down before Optimus Prime and suck on these shiny metallic balls."

His eyes bulging in shock, Charlie grabbed at Left-Nut, but it was too late. Upstairs, the song had ended right as Trent paused banging on the pots to open a beer. Left-Nut's corny shtick might as well have been an air raid siren. Two zombies immediately crashed through the front window and became tangled in the blinds while dozens of others jockeyed for access behind them.

Russ entered the hallway and immediately emptied his pistol, dropping the two lead zombies. However, they brought the blinds down with them and opened a clear path for the others to stream in.

Charlie raced to the kitchen with the type of speed that life and death situations call for. He grabbed the table, tilted it vertically and shoved it into the doorway all in one fluid motion, catching the impact of the racing horde. It inched backwards, and hands poked through the opening.

Russ put his shoulder into the table, pushing it back and pinning the flailing arms snuggly to the wall. "Dammit, Left-Nut, get over here!" he yelled and peered over his shoulder, just in time to see two feet disappearing through the window. "Motherfucker!"

The pair wouldn't be able to hold the crowd back for long, so Charlie pointed to the refrigerator. "When I say go, tip it towards me."

"But—"

"Do it, I'll move," Charlie assured him. "Now go."

Russ pushed the fridge over, and it broke the legs off the table and slammed to the ground, barricading the door perfectly. As Charlie hopped backwards, an object flew off the top of the fridge and hit him square in the chest.

"I found the binoculars."

Chapter 19
The Curious Case of Matt
(Left-Nut) Tucker

"Is it cool to bang a zombie? Like, say it's a really hot one?" Smokey asked and passed his pipe. The outbreak was now a week old and things had slowed down quite a bit. They were spending that particular night gazing at the stars, smoking the last of the pot and focusing on the important things in life.

"No way," Charlie said, a serious look etched on his face. "You're talking statutory rape. A zombie can't give consent any more than a coma patient."

"Or that poor girl Left-Nut recently had sex with," Bruce said and took a hit.

Trent snatched the pipe. "Zombies don't have any rights and you gashes know it. If they did, Cliff could have us shot for crimes against humanity." He threw an empty can at the restrained man who now sported strings of rapidly blinking Christmas lights and a paper sack emblazoned with a smiley face and the words "INSERT PENIS HERE." Cliff looked almost comical in the getup, but his feral grunts betrayed a murderous lust that was just waiting for an opportunity.

"And for the record, if a zombie Jessica Alba were to come shuffling by, I'd feed her a piece of meat all right. Fuckin' quarter-pounder." Trent patted his imaginary giant dong for emphasis.

Mike rolled his eyes. "You know, for me being the only homosexual here, you guys talk about penis an awful lot."

"And that's why we always knew you were a butt pirate, because you say penis," the cop replied. "Real men say cock, shlong, wanker, dong, joint..." Trent's manhood list went on for several minutes.

A lightweight, Bruce leaned back in the lawn chair as his head spun from the designer strain known as New York Diesel. "I'm high as giraffe pussy right now." He squinted at the sky. "Why are the stars so bright? It's like we're out in the country or something."

"Without the smog and city lights, we're close. It seems cooler too," Charlie noted, and he was right.

After a cascading overload of the electric grid, besides Smokey's solar-powered building, Chicago had been dark for days. Without a million air-conditioners dumping out heat, the record temperatures had eased. The gentle breeze would have made for a nice night if not for the stench of rotting flesh wafting in from the neighborhood. It was the turd in the punchbowl nobody wanted to mention.

Bruce sat up. "Did you know Cliff's a sex offender?"

Blake nodded begrudgingly. "Yeah, I knew."

"Why?" Left-Nut said through a split lip and two black eyes, courtesy of Russ and Charlie. They'd threatened to toss the coward off the roof but had settled for kicking the living shit out of him. It was a close vote.

Bruce continued. "True story. We were at a Hawks game and got completely plastered by the second period. This older chick came on to Cliff and blew him right there in the seats. Then the Jumbo-tron picked it up on accident during their kiss-cam shot, and it happened to be family night."

"What happened?" Rob asked and exhaled a monstrous stream of smoke through the air.

"Let's say the judge came down on him way harder than the old skank did."

"That ain't so bad. I've done a lot worse," Russ said and patted Zombie Cliff on the shoulder. "You're still okay in my book."

Cliff's head swiveled towards Russ and shook with anger or hunger. It was hard to tell as the smiley-faced sack made every move look like a well-orchestrated goof. Only Cliff wasn't joking around. He wanted to eat his friends.

Blake sighed. "It was bad. Cliff had to hand out fliers every time he moved and shit like that. He even took a bunch of pills one time trying to kill himself. Poor bastard never did clear his name."

Trent nailed Cliff in the head with another beer can. "I bet he wished he finished the job."

"Stop torturing him," Blake said and rose to his feet. "He might still be in there for all we know. It's not right."

"Oh for fuck's sake, lighten up. He'd treat you like a roast beef sandwich if he had the chance."

Mike turned to Charlie. "You feeling better?"

"No, it still hurts to piss. First time I hook up in four years and I catch something." He punched Blake in the arm. "I never properly thanked you."

The admission blew Russ away. "You hadn't gotten laid in four years in *Chicago*? Talk about no game."

Charlie blinked as he fought the urge to blast back at the mouthy hillbilly. "I was in a rut. The only girl I talked to regularly was the one that cut my hair."

Blake rolled his eyes. "Oh, not her again."

"I called her Tits Magee, for obvious reasons. She was gorgeous, good personality and fun to talk to."

"She got paid to talk to you, dude," Bruce said.

"What happened?" Big Rob asked.

"Absolutely nothing. I got my hair cut every week for a year and never asked her out. I couldn't pull the trigger."

"I always told you to go for it Charlie. Girls with dead-end jobs usually date losers, so you had a chance," Blake said with a snicker.

"Maybe you were better off," Jim said and looked at his feet. "At least you didn't have to lose her. I mean, look at me. I had everything and now I'm sitting in this dump listening to you guys talk about your bullshit problems. I was gonna be a dad, and now..."

Russ's hand crept to the weeping man's shoulder. "Son, life is like a box of chocolates. Only each individually wrapped morsel is really a turd. Some have peanuts, some have corn, but in the end, they're all shit."

"Having kids isn't a big deal anyways. I had about ten running around, and you don't see me crying about it," Left-Nut added with a smug look on his beat up face.

"Shenanigans," Charlie said.

Blake nodded. "This is why you're less popular than dog shit at a picnic, you're always making stuff up."

"Remember that newspaper job I had the summer before junior year?" Left-Nut said.

"How could I forget you trying to sell me a subscription about thirty times?" Charlie said. "You were even more annoying back then."

"Moot point. One day I was covering for a guy at the ad desk and this dude in old timey clothes comes walking in. He was from that weirdo cult south of town."

"The Seventh Day Shepherds? They're like a mix between the Amish and Southern Baptists, only nuttier," Blake said.

Left-Nut nodded. "Yep, that's them. It turned out their gene pool was getting shallow and all their kids were being born with extra fingers and crap. Anyways, they wanted to place an ad for reproductive assistance."

"Like sperm donors?" Russ said and perked up.

"Only they weren't talking test tube babies. It was more of a pinch-hitter situation, if you catch my drift."

"They wanted to pay people to sleep with their wives and get them pregnant?" Mike said.

"Bingo. And since they refused to read the newspaper, like it's idolatry or something, they never knew I trashed the ad. Nobody else showed up, so I was a hot commodity."

"Let me get this straight," Blake said. "You're telling me this religion thinks newspapers are taboo, but a random dude banging their wives is kosher?"

"Crazy, I know. Even better, I got paid five hundred a pop. It was the scam of the century."

Russ beamed with approval. "Impressive. But how'd they look?"

"Like total sasquatches because of all the birth defects. But there was one chick that was hot, and I mean *hot*, and I was biding my time until I could get my turn at her."

"You just strolled into town and started blasting these chicks?" Bruce said.

"It wasn't exactly spring break. We're talking fully clothed, and their relatives are in the room."

"Awkward," Jim added. A rare smile crept onto his face as he listened to the ridiculous story.

"Yeah, I wasn't supposed to show pleasure or make any noises or I'd get fired. Plus, they just lay there, stiff as a board, so it wasn't as awesome as it sounds."

"Oh yeah, you impregnating mutant women while their troglodyte family watches sounds like a regular dream come true," Mike said.

Left-Nut shrugged. "At the end of the summer I finally got a crack at the hottie, and she ended up being the preacher's daughter, go figure. But the thing was, I took a bunch of my dad's Viagra that day because these chicks were seriously testing my libido, and that's saying something because I would pretty much nail a mud puddle."

"No shit," Blake said.

"I'm packing some serious steel that this girl's bum-fuck husband Jedediah or whatever has never done, and she actually opened her eyes, and I can tell she's loving it."

The group stopped their pestering questions and leaned in, lost for a moment in the epic tale. "As if on cue, the storm that was brewing all day crashed into the little cabin. We're talking heavy winds, rain, thunder and light-ning. It was something right out of a movie. Not a porno, mind you, but like a sexy thriller. Maybe something with Brad Pitt." Left-Nut paused and looked at his friends slyly. "But you guys don't want to hear the rest of it since I'm always making crap up."

A collective groan went up in response. "Fine, fine. So there we are, missionary style, literally, because these weirdoes were missionaries. And I started railing this chick and she screams out, 'Oh God, give it to me!'

"I bet they didn't like that," Blake said.

"Yeah, it turns out that was the absolute worst thing to say to The Seventh Day Shepherds, and her family decided to yank the plug on the whole operation. Her husband started crying like a little bitch, and her dad tried to pull me off, but as you can imagine, I was buried in deep as a tick. They paid me to get that girl pregnant, and for once in my life, I was a workaholic." Left-Nut looked around. "Is there any pot left?"

"Finish the damned story," Charlie said.

"They started hitting me on the back with a broomstick, and that just made me pump away harder because I like the rough stuff, but then *wham*! Her dad cracked me in the head with a chair and I tumbled out of bed, bare-assed and pants at my ankles, boner dragging on the floor. So I crawled outside, and by this time half the town's come to kick my ass."

"That, I believe," Mike said.

"I couldn't make it to my car, so I pulled my pants up and grabbed this old bike from the porch. It was like this old 1800's style with metal wheels. Now it's pouring rain by this time and all these inbred dumb-fucks are chasing me on foot. I'm riding up this big ass hill and barely making headway on account of it being such a retarded bike. I got to the top and it was all downhill from there, so I turned to give the dipshits a double middle finger salute. But as I did, there was a huge flash of light."

"There is a God," Jim said dryly.

Left-Nut rose from his seat. "Next thing I know, I'm in the hospital, my hair's permanently turned white, I got black eyes, a broken nose, and my shlong's all bandaged up." He dropped his pants to reveal a giant, solitary testicle gleaming in the moonlight. "And that, dear ladies and gentleman, is how I really earned my nickname."

The group shielded their eyes or turned away in disgust, which allowed Cliff to break free of his bonds unnoticed. Amidst half-hearted cheers, Left-Nut bowed to his audience, completely unaware of the infected lunatic lurching towards him. The brown paper sack fell to the ground, smiley face up, peering at the shining stars overhead.

Chapter 20
All Along the Watchtower

Marquell held aloft the severed head of the hated prison guard, Steve, and addressed those before him. Thick, coagulated blood dribbled from dangling veins with each gesture the maniac made. "Now that I have your motherfuckin' attention, I'm gonna get right down to business. It's simple. I'm the man, and anyone who doesn't toe my motherfuckin' line is gonna get a dome shot."

There were uneasy grumbles among the prisoners, but nobody stepped up to challenge the proclamation. "As of now, the guards, the workers and their families are off limits. Everyone else will keep their old prison job. Motherfuckers on laundry detail are still motherfuckers on laundry detail, and so on."

Juan Garza, a mid-ranking member of the 13th Street Crew, stepped forward nervously while pointing to the guards. "Respectfully, um... why are these *pendejos* getting a free pass? They always treated us like shit."

"I heard that," an armed robber named Dantel agreed loudly. "Their bitches should be up for grabs, right? I mean, a lot of the homies got a piece and I gotta get mine, you feel me? I've been behind bars for five years."

"No. That shit's done," Marquell replied calmly.

"Fuck that! Daddy Longlegs needs some play." Dantel strutted towards the line of cowering and bloodied women.

Marquell merely pointed, and the man's head exploded into a cloud of red mist and gray matter. *Pop, pop, pop.* The rest of the prisoners hit the ground as several more shots sailed harmlessly overhead.

"There's that dome shot I was talkin' about." Marquell waved at the watchtower. "I think y'all know Gus, the crack-shot cracker with an itchy trigger finger? He works for me now. Y'all work for me now." He rolled Steve's severed head like a bowling ball towards the fresh corpse. "Clean this mess up. Shit's ruining my ambiance."

Marquell approached Juan and picked up the discussion without missing a beat. "Now back to your question. Do you know how to run power generators?"

"No *ese*," Juan replied hesitantly.

"What about surgery, or setting a broken leg? No, I didn't think so." The leader turned to the rest of the men. "You see, the only things y'all know how to do is kill and steal. Without me, this place would burn down in a month." He pointed to the electric fence and the dozen or so smoldering zombies stuck to it. "But don't worry, you'll get a chance to do plenty of that. Only it's gonna be on the outside of those walls."

*   *   *

Warden McCabe's eyes opened as his head bounced roughly on the concrete floor. He was being dragged feet first down a corridor in the prison basement, and he couldn't recall how he'd gotten there. A hazy flashback of an ambush on the toilet slowly materialized, and the warden cursed his luck and his taco salad. They stopped.

"This is it, *vato*. Wait here for the boss," one of his former inmates said to another as they dropped the warden's legs to the ground.

"Goddamn!" A crippling pain shot from Jack McCabe's knees to the rest of his body. They had been shattered by repeated blows from a steel pipe.

Footsteps approached, and now it was his turn to wait in fear. He prayed the end would come quickly, but knew better as he recognized the newcomer's voice.

"Get up, you sack of shit." Marquell Washington gave a swift kick to the warden's ribcage. "You said that after you had that animal Steve beat my ass the day I got here, remember? Unfortunately, Steve's no longer with us."

"It was nothing personal, Marquell. I... I had to show the prisoners who was in charge."

"I know that, Jack. I was taking notes the whole time."

The warden had manipulated people his entire life and he wondered if there was an angle to use with his captor. It was doubtful the psycho would listen, but he had to try.

"I actually learned a lot from watching you, Jack, and some of that's gonna help me run this place. For starters, I'll be gettin' acquainted with your wife tonight."

"Please, don't kill her. She hasn't done anything to—"

"Kill her?" Marquell looked bemused at the thought. "She's the hottest piece of ass in the prison, maybe now the entire world. I'm planning to do plenty of things to her, and trust me, killing ain't one of 'em."

The warden continued to brainstorm, believing there was wiggle room for survival if he could only keep the dialogue open. "Don't be rash. I can help you."

"Oh, really? *You* can help *me*?"

"I can tell you where the gold is hidden, and—"

"I don't give a fuck about no gold. I'm not opening a bank." Marquell looked at his newly acquired watch, the warden's shiny Vacheron Constantin. "We're done here, I've got places to be." He pointed to his lackeys. "Toss him in."

The giggling idiots heaved the warden into a dimly lit cell. Jack screamed upon impact and fought the urge to black out. He rolled over to see what was so damned funny.

A severely wounded man came wriggling across the floor towards him, almost slithering. The former deliveryman's tendons had been cleanly cut, but his hunger remained quite intact. Panicking, Jack clawed at the ground and dragged himself away as the zombie closed in.

"I hope you like your roommate."

"No, you can't do this. Please, please!"

Marquell chuckled. "Who's the hamster now, bitch?"

Jack stopped dead in his tracks, not wanting to give Marquell the satisfaction of seeing him struggle any further.

The slow chase ended as the wheezing zombie used its clammy hands to frantically climb up the warden's back. Jack shut his eyes and tried to clear his mind, but there was no happy place to be found when the clumsy attack came. A blind man with a rusty spoon would have done better work.

Marquell's men stopped laughing after witnessing the frenzy of gnashing teeth and squirting veins. A painful reality dawned on them as they viewed the macabre scene; this was the fate of their parents, their girlfriends and their children.

Keeping to his tight schedule, Marquell had them torch the cell and left for his next engagement. Moments later, he arrived outside the private dining room.

Waiting there nervously was one Heather McCabe, a bombshell blonde with long legs, a year round tan and a sense of entitlement. She'd been "asked" to come to the dinner dressed to the nines. The men wielding shotguns were quite persuasive, and having lost contact with her husband after the riot, Heather was in no position to argue.

Marquell leered at her for a full thirty seconds, and then led the knockout by her manicured hands into the room. The floor shifted slightly as they entered, and Heather looked down to see rough plywood had been placed over the mahogany floor.

They sat at a long table as several of the prison "sisters" placed silverware and filled glasses of water. Heather swore she heard a strange whispering noise every time the flamboyant men returned.

Marquell made awkward small talk while picking at overcooked smokey-links and undercooked mashed sweet potatoes. Unfortunately, his vision of high-class women stemmed from watching one episode of *Desperate Housewives*, and Heather was far too preoccupied with survival to humor him.

This woman made Marquell feel like a stuttering schoolboy, which was something he'd never experienced during his countless conquests of hookers, prostitutes and crack-heads. Though the psychopath could literally do with Heather as he pleased, he savored this newfound emotion and desperately wanted her to like him. He pointed downward. "Try the green tomato soup, it goes great with the cornbread I made with my special recipe. I use cayenne pepper to spice it up a notch."

The candlelight glinted off Marquell's shiny watch and Heather immediately recognized that it was her husband's. Her head began to spin and her heart raced. "What have you done with Jack?"

Marquell played with his soup. "This needs to be heated up." One of his fawning attendants spirited the bowls away. Again, the strange noise.

"Please, you need to tell me where my husband is," she pleaded once more, only quieter this time.

Marquell fixed the lovely blonde with a soulless gaze. "He's gone. But I think you already knew that." Her lower lip trembled, and he made his move while she was at her most vulnerable. "Look, I'll tell ya' straight up. You got a choice, are you gonna be my girl, or..."

Heather steadied herself then batted her long eyelashes seductively. "Is that wine I see?"

"Sure is, I made it myself," Marquell said while beaming with pride. "Don't worry, it's made with raisins, oranges and sugar, and I didn't make it in the shitter. I mean toilet," he added hastily.

The former Miss Illinois runner-up poured two glasses of prison hooch and sprouted the fakest smile she could muster under the circumstances. If cozying up to the scumbag meant she'd live another day, the decision was made. Besides, she'd been cheating on her husband with everyone from the UPS guy to her Pilates instructor. In fact, no one would miss Jack McCabe.

Marquell smiled handsomely and clinked his own glass forcefully against Heather's, splashing wine onto the fine tablecloth. Two more servants walked into the room, napkins in hand, and this time an audible groan came from beneath the plywood floor.

Unlike Heather, the surviving gang leaders had refused Marquell's ultimatums. Carlos "The Spider" Huerta, Max "Dime-bag" Dixon and Javonte Taylor found themselves crammed underneath the makeshift floor, bound and gagged. These unlucky dinner guests now suffered a fate Marquell dreamed up while poring over *The History of Attila the Hun.*

The floor compressed further as each extra pound came into the room, pushing air from lungs, cracking ribs and squeezing organs. Heavy tables and chairs, the diners, the food and the servants all added up until the bound men's eyes burst from the pressure. The whispering noises had been fruitless gasps for air and the final death rattles of Marquell's foes. They should have toed his motherfuckin' line after all.

Chapter 21
Sausage-Fest

Big Rob pinned the deadish, snarling beast down and rubbed its face into the gravel. "He doesn't like Left-Nut."

"It's a good thing that I pulled Cliff's teeth or he would've gobbled his last nut down like a chicken nugget," Trent added and pointed his pistol at the back of the thing's head. "But this fuckstick's done for. We can't have Left-Nut shitting his pants every week. Even I think that's messed up."

Mike intervened. "Hold off. We're learning too much from him."

"Like what, that he wants to eat us? Sorry, but that's pretty much Zombie 101, and I don't think we need to keep Cliff around for that type of brilliant insight," Trent replied.

"He's dropping weight."

"So? We're all starving," Bruce said and chuckled, still buzzing from the weed.

"Watch." Mike grabbed a chunk of cat food from an opened can and dropped it under Cliff's slobbering mouth. The zombie completely ignored it.

Trent shrugged. "I don't want to eat that crap either."

"This shows they only want human flesh, and there's not much of that left in the city," Mike said. "If he starves to death, we'll know how long the others can last without food."

"That's all fine and good, except we're gonna starve right along with them," Blake said. "Our stash might last a few more weeks, then what?"

"Then we get more," Mike replied.

Trent holstered his gun. "Okay, so the shit-bag gets a reprieve. Now what are you gonna do with him?"

Mike walked to the side of the roof facing the fenced-in alleyway and pointed downwards. Seconds later, Cliff bounced off of the garbage cans and then rose, seemingly unscathed by the thirty-foot drop.

Russ peered over the edge. "That dude's like a cockroach."

Mike rubbed imaginary dirt from his hands. "Problem solved. Now we can safely study him."

Left-Nut was having none of it. "This is bullshit. That's the second time he tried eat me."

"It is bullshit," Charlie said while holding back a smile. "He should've gotten you the first time."

The excitement over and the group completely out of weed, everyone turned in for another sleepless night. Meanwhile, unaware of his freshly shattered ankle and broken nose, Cliff stared aimlessly at the alley gate like a dog waiting to go outside.

*　　*　　*

The next day began uneventfully. There were angry complaints of hunger, Rob stunk up the place by dropping a ridiculously large dump and the gang turned to self-medication of the alcoholic variety.

"I'm starting to feel like Anne Frank up in here," Blake said as he paced from the living room to the kitchen. For a guy who'd always been on the move, being cooped up was pure torture. It didn't help that chugging whiskey straight from the bottle while watching season ten of *The Golden Girls* was the only entertainment available.

"Not to mention this is a never ending sausage-fest," Left-Nut added, then looked at Mike. "And I bet you're loving it." Mike rolled his eyes and Left-Nut waved his finger. "See? You're eye-fucking me right now."

"And *Golden Girls?*" Blake said. "I can't believe you took the time to grab *that* when you were supposed to be looking for food and medicine downstairs."

"Rue McClanahan has always given me wood for some reason. I think it's because my grandma was sassy and—"

"Shush, I hear something outside," Charlie said. Sure enough, a faint buzzing noise approached from the west. It was a running engine, and the first they'd heard in days. The group raced to the roof with the fragile hope of rescue taking hold.

Blake peered down the street with the binoculars. "It's a school bus, and it's hauling ass."

Charlie grinned at the only good news they'd had. "I subbed at a school about four blocks away that used to be an armory. I bet they were holed up there."

The newcomers weren't alone however, and a large mob of the infected streamed behind the bus pied-piper style. Those in the path of the speeding bus became instant steaming piles of road kill.

The guys cheered them on, reveling with each zombie explosion. "Go! Go! Go!" they shouted in unison. But a loud grinding noise rang out as the fleeing vehicle reached the nearest intersection.

Russ, a truck driver of fifteen years, said one word, and their exhilaration turned to dread. "Transmission."

The bus jerked to a stop and the ravenous crowd was upon it, punching and tearing at the doors and windows. Those inside were trapped like divers in a shark cage, and there was nobody to pull them to safety.

Jim spoke first. "We need to do something, this ain't right." He got no response. "What if those were your kids?"

"Let's go." Big Rob cracked his neck while hoisting a softball bat. Nobody else stood up.

The numbers on the ground rapidly swelled to at least a hundred with more arriving by the second. Someone fired a small caliber pistol through the window several times, but like the Alamo, every attacker knocked down had two more spring up in its place.

Charlie grabbed Jim's shoulder. "You'll get torn to pieces down there."

He yanked away. "So? You call this living?"

The infected throng breached the rear door of the bus and clamored in. Soon, fretful yelling and thrashing gave way to nothing but cold, painful silence. The men on the roof could only imagine what horrors were happening mere yards away.

Big Rob threw his bat at the crowd and then slumped to the ground, sobbing uncontrollably. Jim simply glared at Charlie. "I can't believe I used to look up to you. You're nothing but a coward."

The words stung because Charlie knew they were true and had been for years. Only now his wavering did more than ruin his career and dating life, it cost actual lives. Even worse, they were children.

Surprisingly, the bus door opened and a short man with a beer belly sprinted out while firing a gun. The forty-year veteran gym teacher was instantly gang-tackled to the ground. But the ruse worked as intended, and as countless zombies feasted upon the organs of the unsung hero, a small child snuck off the bus, unnoticed for the moment.

Rob threw the ladder over the side while the others shouted directions.

"Over here!"

"Yo kid, run this way!"

"No, this way, dumbass!"

But the small boy hesitated, and the mob closed in on all sides. The men couldn't bear to watch and averted their gazes as the child screamed. And screamed. And screamed.

Russ's drunken eyes widened as he snuck a peek. "The little bugger got up in a tree." Indeed, the boy had jumped from a fire hydrant to a low hanging limb, and from there scaled up to the top.

After devouring the old man, the zombies next clawed unproductively at the base of the tree. This caused the kid to scream bloody murder and drew even more cannibals to the scene. If a rescue attempt was suicidal before, a move now would be plain idiotic.

Mike stepped in front of his massive friend. "Don't even think about it. Charlie's right, there's too many and they're too fast. We need to wait till the crowd goes away. Then we can see about helping the kid."

Still blubbering, Rob pulled the ladder up while Jim gave Mike a few choice words and then retreated into the apartment to sulk.

"Why can't the zombies be like the ones in the movies?" Bruce said. "You know, the ones that move so slow you can do your taxes while fighting them."

"Because these aren't undead zombies that are sluggish and corpse-like, they're sick people," Smokey said, still considering himself the ultimate word on the issue due to his vast knowledge of B-rated horror movies. "How many times do I have to tell you that? They've got the ZIV, Zombie Immunodeficiency Virus or something."

Trent rolled his eyes. "Like I said, it's fucking Zombie 101 up here. Where do I drop the class?"

Smokey continued to ruminate about the more delicate points of zombie lore while Charlie's shoulders sagged. Disgusted, he wished he had some kind of brain bleach to rid himself of the day's nightmarish images. Charlie grabbed the ever-present bottle of rotgut from Russ's grubby hand, and amid protests, took a long, deep pull. It would have to do.

Chapter 22
Gone Fishin'

Charlie cast his line over the side of the building and dragged his bait across the street, jerking it now and then like the bass pros did on television. It wasn't likely the enormous rats would notice the tiny chunk of meat over the stench of dozens of bloated bodies, but the mindless repetition kept him occupied for hours on end.

He wiped the sweat off his nose, then drained the last drop of whiskey and chucked the bottle. It was nine in the morning. Of course, Charlie had no clue of the time or even what day it was, and it didn't matter. His schedule was wide open. The end of the world had that effect on one's itinerary.

The constant deluge of alcohol and self-loathing had muddled his mind so much that life before Armageddon was but a hazy memory. This was Charlie's new existence, miserable as it was. At least on the roof he could ignore everyone, zone out and listen to the wind whistling down the deserted streets.

Sometimes it wasn't quiet at all. Every so often the wandering mouths would find prey and the solitude of the dead city would evaporate into frenzied cries of terror. After a few minutes it was back to the peaceful quiet of the grave. But that hadn't happened in a while now.

However, that morning had been anything but peaceful as the trapped child kept screaming his little head off. He'd been there three days, stuck twenty feet up a tree while the zombies milled about below. Drawn by his pitiful wails, they'd smeared the bark crimson with blood and skin as they pawed upwards, grasping for a meal just out of reach.

While Charlie tuned the tragedy out and focused on catching a meal of his own, Smokey came outside for some fresh air. "Dude, what's with the Porky Pig outfit? You're gonna give Mike a heart attack."

Charlie hadn't realized he was naked from the waist down and starting to sunburn. He shrugged and went back to fishing. Skin cancer was the least of his concerns.

"That kid has a set of lungs on him." Smokey picked up the binoculars. "It's a shame he won't shut up, it's only drawing more attention."

"A damned shame," Charlie replied without emotion.

"Okay..." The kind-hearted hippy frowned. "You're kind of being a dick lately." He got no response but continued anyway. "A person can't go much longer than three days without water, and in this heat, even less. I wish there was something we could do."

"I suppose we could shoot him." Charlie began reeling in his line.

The door swung open again and a shit-faced Russ came stumbling out with Left-Nut, Rob and Mike following close behind. "You need bigger bait," Left-Nut said and pointed at Charlie's naked waist. Nobody else laughed. "What're you doing anyways?"

Charlie took his tattered shirt off and wrapped it around his waist. "I'm trying to catch one of those little bastards running around everywhere." Indeed, the bodies littering the streets had led to a regular rat bonanza.

"Corpse-eating, carrion-crawlers sizzling off the George Foremen? Sign me up," Left-Nut said.

Mike plopped down in one of the dilapidated lounge chairs. "They'll take over after we're all gone. Sometimes we euthanized pet rats at the clinic and they'd wake back up in the dumpster. You could hear them shaking around inside the bags. Creepy." He thought about their present situation. "I guess we've seen stranger things..."

Charlie kept reeling in the line. "I can't eat any more cat food." He'd switched to a strictly liquid diet of expired Old Milwaukee's Best and various types of liquor for the last several days, and the hunger was sapping what was left of his will to live.

Already annoyed by his present company, another fit from the screaming child set Charlie off. He walked to the edge of the building and pumped his fist in the air. "SHUT THE FUCK UP AND DIE! GO AHEAD AND JUMP! NO ONE'S COMING TO SAVE YOU! YOUR FRIENDS ARE DEAD, YOUR PARENTS ARE DEAD, EVEN YOUR DOG IS DEAD!"

Tears in his eyes, he swore for another minute before quieting to a mumble. Whether from exhaustion or taking a cue from Charlie, the child's screams stopped. Everyone stood in silence.

"I guess he got the message," Left-Nut said.

With the outburst over, the men went back to their normal routines. Alcohol was consumed in mass quantities, dumb jokes were told and laps were swam in the kiddie pool. It was the orgy of stupid they'd become accustomed to. But with food and alcohol supplies dwindling rapidly, the party would be over soon — as in days, not weeks.

Things wound down by mid-afternoon with everyone seriously drunk or passed out. Charlie himself dozed off, fishing pole in hand, when a nightmare took root in his mind. Random images assaulted him including flickering strobe lights, chomping teeth, crawling insects and O.J. Simpson in drag. It was almost bland considering their new reality. Still, Charlie snapped awake and blinked as he tried to remember where he was. The fishing pole wrapped around his wrist started dragging him from the chair. "Holy shit, I got one," he said and roused his friends from their inebriated slumber.

Left-Nut looked over the edge and slapped him on the back. "Looks like a keeper."

Charlie began reeling the wriggling beast in and was careful not to break the line. His friends peered down, anxious to spy the catch of the day.

Mike's smile disappeared as his attention shifted from the dangling rat to something across the street. "That's not good." He pointed to a familiar figure next to the vacant school bus.

The attractive brunette was tall and slender, tanned and toned. But something was off as she stood staring into the sun without a care in the world. A sudden gust of wind rustled her hair and revealed a deep gash creeping from the nape of her supple neck to her collarbone.

Charlie dropped his fishing pole off the roof as his mouth fell open, recognizing the woman he'd known for a decade. Her name was Cindy, and she was Jim's wife.

"I don't remember her tits being so big. Man I'd like to—" Left-Nut's sentence was cut short as Big Rob grabbed him by the throat and applied serious pressure.

"Not another word," Mike said with a glare, and Rob released his death grip on the cretin's windpipe.

"What are you gawking at?" As if on cue, Jim emerged from downstairs. He'd skipped the day's festivities to sleep and was now looking to blow off steam.

Charlie searched for a cover story as the others acted nonchalant. "Oh nothing, I'm heading inside to try a new recipe I've been thinking of. How do you think the Friskies Sea Captain's Choice would taste with hot sauce?"

Jim could tell something was amiss and wondered if he was about to get punked. It wouldn't have been the first time. "Did you guys sneak food out here or something? You better not be holding out on me." He tried to pass by his friends but they formed a line and stopped him. Now it was obvious something was up. "All right, what's the deal?"

Rob and Mike looked at their feet as Left-Nut started chuckling nervously. Charlie stepped forward, his palms facing upwards. "Jim, the thing is... shit, I don't know how to say this. The thing is..."

Confusion crossed Jim's face. "Come on, spit it out."

There was no sugarcoating the situation. "I guess there's something you need to see." Charlie turned towards the street. "But try to stay calm..."

Jim walked to the edge of the roof and looked around, not seeing anything out of the ordinary. Some bodies, some zombies, a lot of trash. Then he noticed the woman and his heart nearly leapt from his chest.

There was his wife, looking beautiful as ever. Denial kicked in and he panicked. "We gotta get her. She won't last a minute if those bastards see her!"

Charlie realized this wasn't going to end well as hysteria took hold of his best friend. He'd have to talk some sense into Jim, and he'd have to do it fast. "There's nothing we can do man. She's—"

Wild eyed and furious, Jim shoved Charlie hard into the wall. "You talked me out of getting her in the first place, not again." He grabbed the thirty-foot ladder but struggled to move it.

Rob put him in a bear hug as Mike spoke calmly. "Put it down and take another look."

He tried to resist, but Rob increased the pressure. After struggling fruitlessly, Jim threw the ladder down with a clang. Reality slowly and painfully clawed its way back.

Mike repeated himself. "Take another look."

Jim saw his lovely wife, the mother of his unborn child, standing in the same spot. But this time he noticed her gaping neck wound. He saw her stiff body swaying slightly with the wind. Finally, he noticed her vacant stare and empty eyes, gazing into nothingness. Jim took one last look at the love of his life, closed his eyes and plunged head first over the side of the building.

Chapter 23
Man Overboard

Big Rob stared in horror at the lone shoe in his hand. Jim had slipped out of his grasp and now lay below, broken and battered on the sidewalk. His arms and legs were bent at awkward angles and a trickle of blood began to pool next to him on the ground.

Other than a gentle rustling of leaves, it was completely silent. Until Left-Nut opened his big mouth. "I always said she'd drive him to suicide."

Charlie briefly entertained the idea of heaving Left-Nut over the side as well, but a faint groan coming from Jim stopped his murderous thoughts. The group sprung into action as Mike whispered out orders. "Lower the ladder, and do it quietly. Jim's a goner if one of these shit-heads hears us." He looked at Rob. "Can you carry him up?"

"I'm on it," Rob said with confidence then lowered the cumbersome ladder. It came to rest on the ground with a scrape, but none of the nearby cannibals noticed.

"Be careful," Mike said. "If his neck's injured and you jostle him, it can cause permanent damage."

Rob nodded, swung his large frame onto the ladder and began the descent. He was halfway down when Jim came to and screamed in agony, unmindful of the danger lurking mere yards away.

"He needs to hurry," Trent said as a pizza delivery boy, a mailman and a naked office worker made a beeline for Jim. Seeing the urgency, Rob plummeted the rest of the way down and crashed into a heap. He rolled to his feet and gingerly scooped Jim up like a baby.

Meanwhile, Trent haphazardly unloaded his clip, missing several times before taking the pizza boy out with a lucky shot to the chest. The pimple-faced teen's heart exploded into a spray of scarlet that hung briefly in the air like a macabre firework. "Eat it, fuck-nut," Trent said and chose his next target.

The rest of the guys hurled anything within reach to slow down the charging pack, including bricks, a rubber football, a cactus and an empty propane tank. With no time to spare, Rob tossed Jim over his back and sprinted up the ladder. Bouncing like a ragdoll, Jim passed out again as his shattered bones cracked and splintered into surrounding tissue. Warm blood from multiple compound fractures streamed down Rob's chest and onto the aluminum steps, causing him to lose his footing.

Cindy latched onto one of Rob's feet, yet the giant advanced anyways, lifting her into the air as he climbed. He tried to shake her off, but the ravenous woman held tight and Rob now supported an extra two hundred and fifty pounds of husband and wife.

As if things weren't bad enough, the nude office worker crashed into the base of the ladder with a bang, tipping it to the side. Charlie and Blake dove in unison and grabbed hold of the ladder right before it could slide out of reach. Nowhere near as strong as he'd once been, Rob started to lose his grip.

Trent reloaded and drew a bead on a spastically shaking Cindy. He squeezed off a single round, and it grazed Rob's shoulder, ricocheting off the pavement.

"Ow!" Rob bellowed.

"Sorry." Trent aimed again and fired. Head shot.

She'd wanted to be a mom for years, and after several rounds of fertility treatments, she was finally going to be. But all the organic food, child-rearing books and classical music had been for naught. Cindy's lifeless body twitched as her diseased brain shut down. A childhood memory of apple picking flickered briefly in her mind, and then she lay still.

The hungry mailman took no notice as he tread roughly on the fresh corpse, his arms reaching skyward, uncaring and oblivious to the tragedy underfoot.

Rob finally struggled to the top and then slumped to the ground, puking. A little more strain and the big man's heart would have burst. Mike and Charlie gently eased Jim down on a wool blanket while the others yanked the ladder up.

"Ugh, he shit himself," Left-Nut remarked as the smell became too obvious to ignore.

Mike did a quick triage. "That's the least of his problems. He's hemorrhaging badly and has broken bones too."

"What can we do?" Charlie asked with desperation creeping into his voice.

"There's only one thing I know of that might stop the bleeding..." Mike paused to take a deep breath. "Plug in the iron."

*   *   *

Charlie still had the noxious odor of singed human flesh in his nose two days later. Stopping the bleeding hadn't solved all of Jim's problems though, and he'd fluttered in and out of consciousness ever since, ranting and raving in between. At one point, he repeatedly said phonebook for six hours straight, alternating between saying it slowly and spitting it out. Whispers, shouts, English accents, it didn't matter; Jim was stuck in a loop. His friends had passed the pity stage and moved right on to annoyance. Of course, some were more annoyed than others.

"Let's end it," Trent said while pissing off the roof and aiming for Zombie Cliff. For his part, Cliff was oblivious to the daily golden shower and meandered around the alley.

"Yeah, I haven't slept in days," Left-Nut added.

Charlie didn't like the harsh tone of the conversation and turned to Mike for answers. "You've been pretty mum, what's the deal?"

"Listen, I'm only a vet, and a pretty crappy one at that. Still, it's obvious we're not talking about a happy ending."

"He said happy ending—"

"Shut the fuck up Left-Nut," Mike said. "Anyways, Jim has serious issues to contend with. Even in a hospital with all modern medicine had to offer, he'd be struggling."

"There's nothing you can do?" Charlie said.

"Look, I have Band-Aids and half a bottle of hydrogen peroxide, and Jim has a broken neck. What the hell do you want from me?" Mike regained his composure. "He's going to get sepsis any day."

"Sepsis? Sounds like a heavy metal band," Russ said.

"It's blood poisoning. And I don't picture him regaining consciousness again. I'm sorry." As if to add emphasis to Mike's diagnosis, Jim started shouting again.

"Sounds like the great communicator's up," Russ said. "Between him and the damned kid, we might as well have a battle of the bands up here."

"Yeah, and more noise means more of these idiots keep showing up," Bruce added.

Charlie paced back and forth. "What do we do?"

"We help Jim find peace. That's what he was trying to do anyways, and—"

"Why didn't we let him die then?" Left-Nut said.

"We did the right thing by trying to save him, now we need to let him go," Mike said. "Bruce is right. If he keeps yelling, we'll have half the city here."

"Do we draw straws or something?" Rob asked.

"How about Trent? He did the wife and kid, might as well finish what he started," Left-Nut said without a hint of remorse.

"One shot, two kills," Trent replied proudly and gave his obnoxious friend a triumphant fist-bump.

Charlie fixed them both with an icy glare. "I used to think Vidu was socially-retarded, but you two make him look like a prom king. Anyways, he's my best friend, so I should do it." Nobody argued.

Trent held out his pistol, but Mike gently pushed it away. "There's no need for that. I'll grind up the last of the sleeping pills and make a drink. He'll just drift off."

Smokey briskly emerged through the door with an odd look on his face. "Guys, Phonebook Jimmy is awake, and he's talking."

Chapter 24
Grocery List

Richard Daley Prison was running smoothly after the initial bloodletting, mostly because everyone was scared shitless of what Marquell would do next. They had ample reason to be.

"Fore!" The new dictator drove a golf ball two hundred yards off his homemade tee, an inmate buried to his neck. "You're lucky you got an afro, brother," he said to the man who'd carelessly stepped on Marquell's shoes. The previous tee, a food hoarder, hadn't been so lucky in the fluffy hair department, and Marquell had broken two drivers off the bald man's head.

A few swings later and Marquell had ruined another driver, made a mess of those same white shoes and run out of balls. He'd made his point, though, and left the yard for the daily boardroom meeting.

Various lieutenants and lackeys packed the room while hoping to melt into the background. Marquell did a roll call then spent an hour going over various administrative tasks, including food preparation, burial detail and setting up a basketball league complete with lady-boy cheerleaders and a playoff system. After stacking his own team with two former NBA players, he dismissed the bulk of the group and waved those remaining to come forward.

The pack of scoundrels glanced around nervously while Marquell whispered to his new second in command, a Columbian hitman by the name of Fausto. The Medellin Cartel *sicario* sported a chest tattoo that had often been confused for the Virgin Mary, but actually depicted Maria

Anuxilatra, Virgin of the Assassins and patron saint of murderers. He'd earned the ink a hundred times over.

Marquell addressed his men with a deep baritone voice. "All right, y'all, I'm gonna keep it one-hundred with you, and I ain't gonna play. Shit's gonna be dangerous. You're gonna smash and grab and bring me back what I want. And think — no cops to worry about."

"Yeah, we have to worry about the devils instead," a prisoner said quietly.

Marquell pointed to the swarthy-looking Fausto. "I'd be more worried about the *loco hombre* right here if you screw up. You feel me? There's a Costco warehouse five miles out where you'll load up one of the buses with supplies. Canned goods, batteries, medicine... and I can't motherfuckin' stress this enough, dog food." He winked at his newfound love interest. "What kind you need again, girl?"

Heather rubbed her teacup yorkie's tiny head and spoke as if she were addressing a child. "Toby's a special little boy, so no generic stuff. He won't touch it if it's not organic."

"You heard her, Toby gets the good shit. Now don't fuck this up or you'll be headed right back out. Remember, this ain't vacation, so don't be getting high or drunk. Oh, and if someone gets bit, blast 'em. Now roll out."

Marquell looked to his dangerous protégé as the ragtag band of rapists, thieves and murderers shuffled out of the room to an uncertain fate. "Think they'll make it back?"

"I doubt it. They seem dumber than the first ones."

Marquell nodded. "Less mouths to feed." He looked at Heather and added hastily, "But if they don't come back, I'll get the food myself, baby girl." He smiled widely. "The things we niggas do for white women."

Heather rolled her eyes while Fausto chuckled. "*Sí.*"

"But back to earlier, I still don't know about half of these guards. I don't want to get blindsided." Marquell's blanket amnesty had held up so far, but friction between the jailors and inmates was growing by the day. Several assaults on guards' wives had gone unsolved and unpunished, and their complaints had grown louder.

"They'll do as they're told. We have favorite saying in Colombia. *Plata o plomo.* It means you can take the silver or take the lead."

Marquell nodded. "True that. But I think we should bring girls in after we get supplies tightened up. Otherwise this shit's gonna get worse. Nothin' more dangerous than a brother with a hard-on. Speaking of," he said and grabbed Heather's well-formed backside. She smacked him hard across the face in response. Marquell grinned. "That's how I like it."

Chapter 25
Pillow Talk

Charlie crept into the bedroom and found Jim sprawled on a dirty mattress, covered with Star Wars bed sheets and a wet rag. Two coat hangers and the ever-ubiquitous duct tape held his head stable to avoid any further damage — not that it mattered.

Jim's papery skin was practically translucent and an overpowering stench of the dying filled the room. Charlie mustered a brave face as every instinct told him to turn and run out. "Hey, bud," he said casually.

"Hey, Charlie," Jim answered, slowly and with effort.

"How're you feeling?"

"Dizzy... and I can't move."

Charlie grabbed Jim's worthless hand. It was cold and clammy and made him want to puke, but he held it tightly just the same. "Are you in much pain?"

"No, I can't really feel anything. Smokey said I made a mess of my legs?"

"You busted 'em up good. But let's not talk about that. Let's relax and talk about something a little more... nice."

Jim nodded. "Here's something nobody's mentioned in a while, but do you remember that time Vidu kicked a girl?"

"I'm the one that yanked her off him. He was screaming, 'I kill you bitch! I kill you bitch!' And the girl was waving a handful of his hair around like she'd scalped him."

"God, his English was horrible back then," Jim said and cracked a smile.

"It didn't get much better. Vidu never could remember what to call nachos. Dumbass kept calling them Cheetos for some reason. And of course, that wasn't the last time he got a beat-down from a girl," Charlie said, recalling the bachelor party prank that seemed to have happened in a different lifetime.

"He had trouble adjusting over here... but we did make his life better, I think, even if we always busted his balls."

Vidu was probably wandering the streets of Chicago at that very moment, much like Jim's wife had been, so Charlie moved on. "Hey, how about that time my mom caught Left-Nut jerking off into the campfire on the Fourth of July? What a creeper."

"Hah, that was awesome." Jim paused to cough, and bloody foam trickled down his gaunt chin. "Those pool parties were great, weren't they?"

"Ice-cold kegs, a badminton court complete with dog-crap obstacles, a fire-pit, topless hour and teenage girls, yeah, they were legendary." They'd also been Charlie's high water mark, and everything had gone downhill since.

"If you couldn't get laid there, you just couldn't get laid," Jim said wistfully.

Charlie didn't remember Jim landing anyone at the parties, but let it slide under the circumstances. He was about to kill the poor guy after all. "I wish that summer never ended. We were like kings or demi-gods or something. Not to sound gay, but it was magical."

"It had its time and place, but you can't live in your mom's basement forever. We all had to grow up. We all *should* have grown up," Jim added pointedly.

Charlie nodded, knowing his Peter-Pan Syndrome had made him miserable for the last decade. "I don't know why, but I just couldn't move forward."

Jim's mood darkened. "I guess now it doesn't matter who was successful or important. Who was happy..."

"That's not true. You had something special going with Cindy that most people never had, and that counts for something. I sure as hell didn't have it. Trust me, we were all jealous."

Jim made a face. "What's that smell anyways?"

"I think Rob's stinking up the place again," Charlie said. "You know how he normally is, and now he's eating cat food twice a day."

"The big oaf really saved me?"

"Rob went over the roof like a banshee in a blender. I haven't ever seen him move that fast when food or beer wasn't involved."

"He's always been a good guy. You need to take care of him for me."

"You can help me when you get better. It's just gonna take some time for your bones to heal up. Mike has a rehab plan in place and we're gonna have you kicking a soccer ball by the end of the year." The white lies were getting ridiculous but Charlie didn't know how to stop at this point. He made eye contact. "Jim, you were always my ace in the hole when I needed you, I'll never forget what you did for me all these years."

Jim looked uneasy. "No, I was a pretty big scumbag at times. You should know I wasn't always loyal."

Curious, Charlie leaned forward. "Okay, fill me in." Jim had always been fairly milquetoast, so he assumed a bland tale of stolen beer was coming his way. He was wrong.

"Do you remember that Halloween party sophomore year? We served hundreds of Jell-O shots to the sororities while that crappy cover band played."

"I remember some of it. Everything got hazy after I bonged a pitcher of rum and coke and snorted a bunch of Vivarin. I could have died that night."

"Carrie Evans and I took care of you after you streaked through the party and passed out in the shower," Jim said.

"I vaguely remember that."

"We kept you on your side and made sure you puked in the trash can all night."

Charlie wasn't following him. "I had the hangover of the century after that. But how does taking care of me make you a bad friend?"

"Look, despite how shitty you treated her, everyone knew you loved Carrie."

"True," Charlie replied, arching an eyebrow. His complex relationship with the stunning girl had gone from drunk-dialing booty-calls to genuine feelings, but it eventually fizzled out due to Charlie's fear of commitment. The two never reached closure, and Charlie still regretted how things merely faded away after graduation.

"The thing is... she was dressed like a slutty racecar driver that night."

"I remember that outfit." Charlie wondered if maybe Jim wasn't so milquetoast after all. "Go on."

"We were both totally bombed and it got late, you know, and, and..."

"And?"

"I banged her," Jim said quickly. "You slept right through the whole thing." He looked like a dog that had been kicked by its owner.

Charlie gazed at his paralyzed friend for a few awkward seconds. Jim had betrayed him and the revelation stung. He cleared his throat and then chuckled softly. "You randy little turd." Had the information come a few days earlier, Charlie would have taken him to the woodshed and not felt a bit sorry for it. As things were, he could only laugh it off.

"You mean... you're not mad?"

"I'm trying to picture you two going at it with me lying in my own puke. How romantic." Charlie knew Jim didn't fully believe him, probably because it was bullshit. Still, he put up a good front. "Look, I wasn't going out with her and that was my fault. I had years to ask her out and didn't. I wanted the cake and some pie on the side. It's the story of my life, I can't step up."

"True, but I shouldn't have done what I did. It was a tool move and—"

"No you shouldn't have, but at this point who really gives a shit? I know I don't, and I know you shouldn't. It's water under the bridge Kemo Sabe, and besides, I need to come clean too. It isn't quite the same kind of bombshell, but do you remember how your room always smelled horrible senior year?"

It was Jim's turn to look puzzled. "Yeah, I had some maintenance workers there every week trying to figure out why. They thought maybe a dead mouse was in the walls."

"It wasn't a mouse. I'd sneak in there and piss down the radiator vents when I was drunk. Sorry, I didn't really have a reason. Just thought it was funny."

"I always thought it smelled like piss. Anyways, I'm glad I got that off my chest. Now on to the serious stuff. Will you pray for me?"

"I'm not a religious man, and especially not after the past few months," Charlie said.

"It doesn't matter. You know I was an altar boy right?"

"Yeah."

"But did you know I got molested?" Jim asked.

"Oh man, I'm sorry to hear—"

"Nah, I'm messin' with you." Jim laughed, and dark, thick blood ran out of his nose. Charlie wiped it off and Jim continued. "But seriously, I'm scared about going to hell. Suicide's a mortal sin after all."

"If there's a hell, you're not going there. Even if you did nail Carrie Evans behind my back, you sneaky son of a bitch." He squeezed Jim's dead hand. "Besides, you didn't kill yourself and you're gonna be fine."

The two talked for hours until Jim's voice grew soft and he wasn't making much sense. Charlie had delayed the inevitable, but the charade was over. "I think it's time you get some rest." He grabbed the deadly cocktail. "This'll help you doze off." The twenty ground-up Triazolam tabs were enough to put a rhino to sleep.

He poured the solution down Jim's throat, careful not to spill a drop. Still, after several minutes of sleep, Jim's body shuddered and he puked most of it up. There were no more pills, and Charlie hoped it had been enough. Jim's pulse slowed and his breathing drew shallow as the end seemed near. Then he snored. Loudly.

"You gotta be shitting me," Charlie said and grabbed a pillow. He took a deep breath, closed his eyes and applied firm pressure to his friend's motionless face. He held it there for a minute and then slumped to the floor amidst dirty socks and dust bunnies.

Jim was finally at peace with his eyes closed, a relaxed jaw, and the faint hint of a smile on his resting face. "Phonebook!" he shouted out and gasped for air.

Charlie panicked and pressed the pillow down so hard his arms trembled and cramped, and there would be no waking up this time. His tears saturated the Superman pillow as he used it to kill his best friend. Heartbroken, Charlie closed Jim's vacant eyes and covered him with a sheet. Then he opened his dresser drawer and pulled out two items he'd hidden away for years.

Chapter 26
White Lightning

Left-Nut adjusted his binoculars and leered at the once gorgeous but now mangled jogger. "That's right, you dirty little gutter-zombie. Bend over and let Dr. Tucker take your temperature. Oh, it's your first time? That's okay, I'm a trained professional and I always—"

Charlie burst through the door and interrupted the private moment on the roof. "That'll make you go blind," he said while walking to the edge and peering across the street.

"I happen to have a medical condition that requires... hey what's with the getup?" Left-Nut said when he noticed that Charlie sported an ill-fitting spandex track uniform and running shoes, circa 1998. "Going for a jog, are we?"

"Actually, yes." He struggled to lift the ladder.

"I see." Left-Nut ran to the door. "Guys, get up here, Charlie's going Charlie Sheen on us."

Soon the whole gang came topside. Mike spoke first. "Care to explain yourself?"

"Sure. Jim's dead, and we're all a bunch of pussies," Charlie stated pointedly.

Mike frowned. "Calm down and let's talk it out."

"I can't keep living like this. Cowering around, not even helping a child. We're no better than the cannibals. Hell, we're worse, because we should know better."

"What're you gonna do, tough guy?" Trent asked.

"I'm gonna be a man for once. Big Rob, a little help?"

Rob hoisted the ladder over the side and gave a proud nod to his friend while Mike tried to intervene. "Okay, but we need a plan."

"The kid's been up there too long already." With that, he climbed down. Charlie's adrenaline pumped furiously as he crouched towards the middle of the street, but what came next was surprisingly anti-climactic. There weren't any charging hordes, no screaming ambushes, nothing.

"Big deal, I could've done that," Left-Nut said.

Charlie reached the tree, still unnoticed, and whispered up. "Kid, run to the ladder when I draw them away." There was no reply and Charlie's head sunk as a dull lump formed in his stomach. His own words haunted him. "Shut up and die!"

"What's he waiting on?" Russ said as Charlie slunk back towards the apartment.

And then there was movement. Charlie turned to see the kid slowly making his way from the top of the tree. A feeling better than any drug he'd ever taken washed over him — hope.

The former four hundred meter conference champion took a deep breath and made his move. "Fresh meat, come and get it!" A handful of the infected bolted in Charlie's direction without hesitation, and he blasted off down the street as if coming out of starter's blocks.

"Holy crap, has he always been that fast?" Bruce said in disbelief as Charlie left the mob in his dust and easily maneuvered around several creatures coming from the opposite direction.

"They called him White Lightning in college," Blake said. "Before he started drinking every night, then they just called him Second String. It wasn't as catchy though."

Charlie's beer belly stretched the red singlet to its limit and he looked ridiculous, but it felt amazing to open up with the wind whipping through what remained of his once flowing mane. He was alive, dammit, even if only for a few more minutes.

Soon Charlie had made it three-quarters of the way around the block, had dozens of bogeys on his tail and was getting tunnel vision. Unfortunately, a sedentary lifestyle and diet of beer and cat food did nothing to encourage long distance running. Though the zombies lacked Charlie's speed, they didn't feel the pain of burning lungs or lactic acid buildup, and began to close in.

He made the final turn only to see the disheveled kid standing at the bottom of the tree, unwilling to cross the street without an adult. Charlie relaxed his muscles to avoid tightening up and pulled in for the last leg of his most important race. He'd simply scoop the kid up and carry him to safety. No big deal.

Only it wasn't that easy. Upon throwing the child over his shoulder firefighter style, Charlie blew out every muscle in his lower back and tumbled ass over elbows in the process. He heard footsteps and rolled over to buy the child time to escape. The lead zombie, a former cancer patient in a tattered hospital gown, dove for its meal. But it stopped in midair and Charlie blinked, utterly confused.

The mystery was solved as Big Rob spun and power-slammed the man onto a fire hydrant, impaling him in an instant. Blake helped Charlie to his feet while Rob carted the boy to safety.

Meanwhile, Smokey aimed his pistol point blank at another charging man, but the safety was on. Swearing, he fumbled with the gun, only to be saved by a well-placed swing of a baseball bat courtesy of Gay Mike. Mike then followed up with headshot after headshot and knocked several more attackers out of commission in seconds.

Not to be outdone, Bruce tangled up two approaching zombies with a gladiator-like toss of a blanket. Even he was surprised it worked. The rescuers battled their way to the ladder as Trent gave semi-accurate cover fire from the roof. One by one they made it home until Rob pulled the ladder to the top.

Charlie collapsed to the ground, overwhelmed and in pain. "Thanks, guys, I don't know what else to say."

Bruce slapped him on the shoulder. "You don't have to say anything. Seeing you take off like that, it was badass. I guess we got caught up in the moment." He looked at Left-Nut. "Most of us did anyways."

"Somebody had to hold the ladder."

Mike beamed at Charlie. "Jim would have been proud of you. Proud of all of us, actually."

"Yeah, that was something else," Russ said and struck a Marlboro Man pose while lighting a cigarette.

Though it hurt, Charlie sat up and pointed. "Where the hell did you get that?"

"This? Oh, I made a score," Russ said and tossed a trash bag on the ground. "I raided that bar across the street. Great diversion, by the way." The bag was full of cheap cigarettes and grain alcohol.

Trent opened the bag and scowled. "Generics?"

"It's my brand."

"Oh for fuck's sake, did you grab anything to eat at least?" Blake asked.

"Sure did. Food of the gods, beef jerky."

"I can't believe we're related, I really can't," Blake said and tore into a piece of the dehydrated heaven.

The rescued child, a skinny black kid around six years old, chugged down a cup of rainwater and then promptly fell asleep on a folding chair.

"Now what are you gonna do with it?" Trent said.

Charlie ignored the disdain in his friend's voice. "We'll take care of *him*, of course."

"First thing we need to do is get him a fresh set of clothes since these are covered in piss," Mike said. "We'll give him a bath and chow when he wakes up."

"So you wet-nurses are setting up a gay-care center? You know, this is the type of crap we should have talked about," Trent said.

"You think we should have left him there?" Charlie said.

"Why not? That's exactly what we did until you got a wild hair up your ass." Trent wasn't winning anyone over. "I'm just saying, we need a kid like a fish needs a bicycle. And he's a nigglet to boot."

"That's enough of that," Charlie said.

"Hey, Russ, do you know why black guys cry during sex?" Trent asked, picking up steam.

"No." Jerky hung from Russ's mouth like a clown cigar.

"Because of the mace." Trent was so busy laughing that he didn't see the punch coming that totally annihilated him. Rob stood sheepishly over the cop's prone body. Like Charlie, he'd heard enough.

Russ lifted Trent's limp hand in the air then dropped it to the ground. "Dude, I think you killed him." Trent wasn't dead, but he never would remember what happened.

"I'd say he had that coming for, oh, twenty years, give or take and—" Charlie stopped midsentence as a bright light shone into his eyes, and it felt briefly as if God were putting a spotlight on his good deeds. Only it wasn't God.

"Somebody's flashing a mirror at us," Blake said and adjusted the binoculars. He cracked a smile. "This is an interesting development. It's some hot chicks on a roof two blocks down. They're writing on a dry erase board."

Left-Nut perked up as if he'd struck gold. "Spit it out already, what does it say?"

Blake lowered the binoculars. "Starving, need food."

Chapter 27
All Rockets, No Sockets

"I call dibs on the blonde with the monster jugs," Left-Nut said without hesitation.

"Fine by me, I got the redhead." Russ rubbed dirty hands through his greasy mullet. "My third wife was a fire-crotch."

Blake turned to his uncle. "You can't call dibs on what might be the last two women on earth. Besides, didn't your third wife stab you?"

"Oh yeah," he said while giving Left-Nut a high five as if it were a good thing. "Twice. Stitched myself up."

Mike took the binoculars to see what the fuss was about. "They're hot, I'll give you that."

"I knew you weren't all rockets, no sockets," Russ said and patted him on the back.

"I still appreciate the female form from time to time."

Bruce piled on. "Mike is such a breeder. You know he wants to take those girls to pound-town." Sure, it was idiotic to act like Mike was secretly straight, but it passed the time, and that was something they had plenty of.

The fantasies and grab-assery went on for hours since they finally had reason to celebrate. After all, they'd scored a fresh supply of booze and gained the somewhat distant, yet entirely possible, prospect of getting laid. Not to mention Trent was still unconscious, and that in itself was a cause for revelry. They set him in a chair a la *Weekend at Bernie's* and went about their business around him.

But some of the talk turned downright sadistic, even for this group, causing Charlie and Mike to retreat to the kitchen for further discussion. "I know everyone wants to head over and visit the girls, but let's face it, that's setting up for disaster," Mike said quietly, not wanting to wake the sleeping child in the living room.

Charlie nodded. "These guys are walking hard-ons and Trent's becoming more of a lunatic every day, so yeah, we should keep our distance."

"Speaking of Trent, you know he's gonna shoot Rob when he wakes up."

"Not without his bullets," Charlie replied and placed them on the table one after another.

Mike smiled broadly. "Nice move, Chuck. But back to the girls and their food situation. We have to figure out something soon."

"Way ahead of you. I still have a water-balloon launcher we used on spring break to shoot beers from the balcony to the beach. I bet we can toss cans that far no problem. Now aiming it..."

"But do you really think they'll eat cat food?" Mike said. "These girls look pretty high maintenance."

"Sure, it has the consistency of a soggy turd and the re-fined taste of a boiled nut-sack, but they'll make the same choice we did."

"You're really on top of your game today. I'm impressed."

Charlie smiled with atypical pride. "I know, it's like a fog's been lifted or something. I feel great, well, other than my back."

"Sobering up?"

"Yeah, I guess."

"Keep it that way. We need you like this." Mike pointed to the living room. "Especially the kid."

Left-Nut and the others strolled in. "Interrupting your circle-jerk?"

"Need something?" Charlie replied as he hid the ammo.

"Can we look at the little rascal?" Russ said, slurring his speech. The cheap whiskey had done its job and he was feeling no pain.

Mike rose from the table and took on a fatherly tone. "Yes, but don't wake him up."

"Has he said anything yet?" Bruce asked.

Mike shook his head. "I think he might be a mute. Plus he's underweight and dehydrated. But with some t-l-c he should be fine. I think."

They surrounded the child as his chest peacefully rose and fell to the rhythm of life. For a brief moment, each man forgot his own grief, weakness and failure. Lying before them was a symbol of what had disappeared and a vision of what might be again.

Rob gently patted the kid's head and started to bawl, his big body shuddering uncontrollably. Once the floodgates opened up, the others quickly joined in, each crying for a different reason.

Except for Matt "Left-Nut" Tucker, who was always one to ruin a moment. He opened his mouth in a sneer, only to hold his venom tongue and walk out the door. The image of Rob's fist smashing Trent into a bloody pulp had been a powerful one.

Charlie spoke to his sobbing friends. "We did something here, and I'm proud of everyone. Mike's gonna get the little guy cleaned up, and we've got another mission to do."

They dried their eyes and reassembled on the roof while Charlie retrieved the slingshot from under a mountain of junk in his closet. Smokey used his cocaine mirror to signal the girls while the others tried to gauge the distance and the direction of the wind. "I don't think this'll work," Bruce said after realizing how far away their target was.

"Never underestimate these guys when they put their minds to something," Blake said. "Especially if there is vagina involved."

Rob held the two-man launcher steady while Smokey stretched the rubber cables taut at a full thirty feet. Any further and they risked snapping the device and taking someone's eye out. Charlie placed a can of Ocean Delight into the holder and backed up. "Fire away," he said.

Smokey released his grip and the lines snapped forward, smacking Rob in the gut at ninety miles an hour while the can whizzed past his face just as fast. It crashed into the next building over and exploded into a frothy mist of gelled meat by-product.

Charlie grimaced. "Sorry. Angle it up more," he added while reloading. They fired again and sent the projectile far enough but missing wide right.

The girls jumped and waved encouragement from afar, obviously desperate at this point. Realizing this, Left-Nut could not help himself. "Show us your tits!" They didn't.

Four shots later, a can lazily arced over their target and the blonde held it up triumphantly. Having the distance and angle down, they made five of the next eight attempts. Uncle Russ dished out a celebratory round of shots and high-fives.

Charlie abstained and chose that time to broach the root-canal of a subject they'd been avoiding. "Guys, we need to do something about Jim's body. I'd like to bury him somehow. And Cindy, what's left of her, too." The bloated rats of the city had descended on the corpses in the street, skeletonizing them with gruesome efficiency.

"We could drop down into the alley and pull up some bricks. Bury 'em there," Blake said. "Of course we'll have to keep Cliff busy, but that's no big deal."

The idea was a good one and they agreed to carry it out soon. Settling the matter, the gang had an impromptu wake by passing a bottle and recalling their favorite Jim stories, as boring as they were. When it came time for Charlie to speak, he brought up Jim's spicier tale of betrayal, and things quickly got weird. Nobody would look him in the eye, and Left-Nut mumbled something under his breath. Charlie got a familiar sinking feeling. "What's the deal? Did you guys know about this?" He could tell by their shady expressions what the answer was.

Blake gritted his teeth. "Dude, we really hoped you wouldn't find out. But now that you know part of the story you might as well get the unvarnished truth. Everyone nailed your girl Carrie. They didn't call her First Bank because she had a lot of money. That broad took more deposits than Bernie Madoff."

Smokey nodded. "Yeah, she blew Vidu of all people. He was helping her study for a finance exam and the next thing he knew... wham, balls deep!"

Left-Nut clucked his tongue in disdain and swooped in for the kill. "It's pretty sorry when your dream girl banged most of your friends and half the baseball team. And you call me pitiful?"

Charlie's head spun and he tilted forward as his mouth watered. He felt like he'd just discovered he was adopted and Santa Claus was fake all at once. What was worse, the sucker punch came right as he'd regained his confidence. He pitched forward and projectile vomited while his friends lost it.

The howling laughter caused Trent to jump right out of his lawn chair, wild-eyed and dazed. "What the hell just happened?"

Chapter 28
Iron Man

The change in Trent's behavior over the past week had been stunning. Gone were the racist jokes, mean-spirited pranks and random acts of violence. He even stopped pestering Zombie Cliff for the most part. The dirty cop now spent his time scrubbing the apartment and telling stories to the child that he'd named Brandon.

Not everyone believed in the miraculous transformation. "Trent's acting like Martha Stewart, what gives?" Blake said and bit his lip while Mike jabbed him with a shot of insulin. "It's odd."

"Unless you buy into Fred Flintstone lifestyle-changing head injuries, I'd say he's bullshitting us." Mike pulled out the syringe and applied a Band-Aid.

Charlie agreed. "Trusting Trent's like putting your cock in a shark's mouth and expecting a blowjob, you won't be happy with the results. And I find it peculiar that he had exactly eight bullets left."

"One for each of us," Mike said ominously, then changed his tone. "Are you over the Carrie Evans thing? I know that must have been pretty shocking to hear."

"I think all the puking was withdrawal symptoms, but I was upset," Charlie said and chuckled self-consciously. "Still, it wasn't a total surprise."

"Why's that?" Blake asked as he rubbed his arm.

"I showed up at her dorm during finals one night and she was acting weird, like she couldn't wait to get rid of me. I always wondered if someone was hiding in the closet, R. Kelly style."

Now it was Mike's turn to look uncomfortable. "Yeah, about that... sorry."

Charlie's jaw dropped. "Oh come on! I got snaked by a gay guy? You gotta be—"

A loud scuffle in the living room interrupted their chat as Bruce angrily confronted Left-Nut. "Answer me this, why do you smell like cherries? If you're hiding food, I'll—"

"Ginger, you're not gonna do shit," Left-Nut replied calmly. "But if you must know, it's cherry-flavored sex lube. I snagged it downstairs, so when we meet the ladies my breath's gonna be fruity fresh and my dong's gonna—"

Bruce scoffed. "You got the fruity part right."

"Have you smelled *your* breath lately? I'll start calling you Butter-loaf 'cause your teeth are so yellow they could butter a whole loaf of bread."

Russ chuckled and Bruce turned on him in an instant. "You don't have any room to talk with your summer teeth. Some are there, some aren't." The reality was that everyone's hygiene had disappeared since Charlie's travel size toothpaste ran dry, and gingivitis was the least of their problems. A steady diet of cat food and alcohol had led to the early stages of scurvy, and without vitamin C, they'd all be losing teeth. And that wasn't to mention the stench.

Now it was Russ's turn to fire back. "Boy, you got a gator mouth and a gerbil ass." He raised his fists in a challenge.

Bruce stood his ground. "Fuck off, hill-jack."

"Listen up, brother—"

"No, you listen up. Talking like an idiot and having that ridiculous hair doesn't make you Hulk Hogan."

At that moment, Trent entered the fray, carrying the mute child on his back while making airplane noises. He stopped to dish out disdainful looks and words of wisdom. "You're all setting a bad example for Brandon." They rolled their eyes at the man running for step-dad of the year, previously known for shaking down the homeless for coke money. "It's time to grow up and stop bickering. WWJD?"

Russ laughed. "Says the jerk who threatened to rip my mustache off and wipe his ass with it."

"This is too much. Trent used to sneak into everyone's rooms at the frat house and take a needle to their condoms," Blake added.

Trent set the child down gently on the couch. "True, I have behaved poorly in the past, but can't a man change?" Their resounding answer was no.

The circular firing squad kept going until Mike stepped in. "Since we're all here and in such a great mood, we should talk about our next steps."

Now Left-Nut threw his hands up. "Let's hear it, Rambo. Or should I say, Rainbow?"

Mike ignored the white-haired loudmouth as he always did. "This junk we're eating is killing us, and we're about out of it anyways. Not to mention the girls need more food. There's no other option — we have to venture out."

"And I've only got one more day of shots," Blake added. "After that I'm pretty much boned."

Charlie stood up. "I figure we can kill three birds with one stone by going across the street. We'll hit the animal clinic for the drugs, the Halloween store for clothes, and the quick-e mart on the corner for food. The problem's actually doing it."

Trent un-holstered his firearm. "Sounds good, but you'll need a sheriff to lead this posse. Who's got my bullets?" Nobody volunteered, and a dejected Trent sat down amidst the awkward silence.

"We can't go off half-cocked like we did before or we'll get killed," Bruce said. "We need a strategy."

It was at this time that Smokey stood up, rubbing his hands together like a Bond villain. "Luckily for you boners, I've been dreaming about this type of scenario for decades."

"You and every other nerd in America," Left-Nut said with a huff. "But look outside and you'll see some of your fellow zombie fan-boys covered in shit with half of their fucking faces ripped off."

Smokey was unperturbed. "Why do you think I made this doom-stead? I was prepared for bird flu, martial law, economic collapse, alien invasion, you name it."

"Okay, Nostradamus, why didn't you stockpile more food?" Bruce queried loudly.

"I did, but you know I get the munchies a lot." He was unchallenged on that point. "I'm gonna need Big Rob's assistance upstairs for a bit, so the rest of you hang ten."

An hour later, with "Iron Man" on the stereo, Rob came in wearing an ill-fitting snowsuit covered head to toe in duct tape. A Chicago Bears helmet and a rather large sword rounded out the ensemble. His hair flowed out the back and added to the archaic look.

"If it isn't Dildo Baggins," Left-Nut announced wryly.

"He might look idiotic, but someone should try biting him," Smokey said. Left-Nut didn't hesitate to latch on to Rob's forearm like a suckling pig.

"Ow, that hurts, you little buttnugget," Rob said and knocked the jerk down with a cuff to the ear.

Smokey raised Rob's arm for inspection. Sure enough, the tape was slobbery, but intact. "These zombies aren't shit if you take away the element of surprise," Smokey formulated. "Give Rob room to work and he'll plow through 'em like Mike would a bunch of sailors on shore leave."

Charlie started a slow clap. "I gotta ask though, where in the hell did you get a sword?"

"Same place I get all my junk. QVC."

Chapter 29
Elvis Has Left the Building

Big Rob stepped into the corpse-littered street gripping the sword so tightly his knuckles turned white. He'd never even held a sword, much less used one in mortal combat, and his confidence in the plan was shaky at best. Smokey had lost a lot of brain cells over the years after all.

But the worrying ended as soon as the first creature staggered towards him. Oddly enough, it was the freak show Santa from the bike parade, now missing a foot and the lower half of his costume. Rob clumsily thrust the sword at the zombie's jolly mid-section and buried it to the hilt. Santa hit the ground while Rob pulled the bloody blade out, impressed with himself.

"Bad Santa," Russ said from his observation post on the roof, drunkenly chuckling at his own pun.

Rob didn't have time to celebrate as a short McDonald's worker rushed towards him. More confident, he swung for the fences and the single mom's head tumbled into the gutter. It was a rough ending for a woman that worked sixty-hour weeks to put her kids through private school, but this was no fairy tale.

"Highlander, there can be only one!" Russ shouted from afar. Soon, every zombie within earshot joined the rumble and Rob had to backpedal as they swarmed around him.

Using his entire weight, Rob swung wildly and connected. The powerful blow met the thick skull of a tow truck driver and Smokey's Lord of the Rings Collector's Edition sword snapped in half. Out of options, he opened the alley gate with the entire neighborhood following him. In a fluid move for such a big man, Rob hurdled Jim and Cindy's fresh grave and dropkicked Cliff square in the chest, sending the emaciated zombie clattering across the bricks.

The feral mob closed in while biting at Rob's limbs and trying to pull him down. All he could do was toss them off one at a time. But no matter how hard he body-slammed, clothes-lined and karate-chopped, they came right back after him. Thankfully, the ladder touched down and Rob hustled up while his friends hurled insults and projectiles at the raging pack of savages.

The loud commotion brought even more cannibals to the scene and the growing rabble pressed in tighter and tighter while Rob egged them on, just out of reach. Finally, the surprising genius of the plan came into focus as Smokey pulled a rope and the gate swung shut, trapping the mosh pit of zombies inside.

Success. They'd packed in seventy two poor souls like cattle and the streets now appeared empty. After making sure Rob's pseudo-armor held up, the gang climbed down, leaving only a sickly Blake behind to guard the ladder.

Rob led the way, carrying a wooden bat spiked with nails and a brand new attitude. The others huddled behind their battle-hardened "tank" and brandished their own assortment of garden tools, kitchenware, and construction implements. They were just as likely to injure themselves or each other, but desperate times called for desperate measures. Fully exposed, they'd need to rely on stealth and speed to get the goods and return.

Rob farted loudly.

"Damn, hold it in, will ya?" Charlie whispered as they approached the nearby convenience store. In a rare bit of good luck, it was unlocked.

They were used to the smell of countless bloated bodies baking in the sun, but the stench from inside was on a completely new level. Sour milk, moldy fruit, rat droppings and a sticky substance on the floor all combined into a hodgepodge of funk. Mike plugged his nose and waved everyone in. "Remember, quick and quiet."

The men spread out and grabbed whatever their hearts desired most. For Charlie, it was canned peaches and jars of applesauce, while Russ took armfuls of cigarettes and trucker-speed. Of course, Rob went straight for the candy aisle while Left-Nut, still dreaming of future hook ups, snagged shampoo and toothpaste. Oddly enough, Trent hit up the toy section and grabbed balsa airplanes and other junk for his unlikely new best friend. If he was putting on an act, he was doing a great job of it.

Bruce was the most practical of all and searched for Pepto-Bismol and the softest toilet paper he could find. The poor diet had wrecked more than their breath, and these items would be priceless. He tossed economy-sized packs into a shopping cart and moved swiftly down the aisle, but his rusty cart squeaked as he turned a corner, and an eerie sound rose in response from the back of the store.

Everyone froze in place with their weapons at the ready, but no attack came. The store grew quiet once more as Rob strode to the rear like a knight searching for a dragon to slay. "All clear," he whispered. Then he looked at the floor. "Ah, shit."

Charlie rushed to his friend. "What is it?"

Rob pointed and uttered what might be the single most disturbing word in the English language: "Zom-baby." A sickly-looking toddler emerged from the filth and inched its way towards Rob's foot. The starving abomination opened its tiny, toothless mouth and tried to gnaw through Big Rob's sneaker. He didn't have the heart to dispatch the wretched creature. None of them did.

Finally, Russ removed his faded REO Speedwagon shirt and lovingly wrapped the small child up. He disappeared into the deep freezer and shut the door behind him. A minute later, the father of five returned shirtless and visibly shaken.

Charlie tried to cheer him up by pointing to the crude homemade tattoo on Russ's arm depicting the Tasmanian Devil masturbating over a Chevy symbol. "How did that seem like a good idea?"

"You would be surprised what sounds cool when you're huffing spray-paint," he replied and sniffled away tears. "My kids liked it, though."

After regaining their composure, the crew finished up looting the store and gathered by the register for their next move. Charlie noticed a disheveled creature standing in the middle of the road near the corralled zombies. "Rob, you better bring it in before a crowd forms. Curious bastards."

The giant propped the door open and whistled, and the lone zombie ran right into a storm of hacking, slashing, bashing and poking. Even Left-Nut got a lick in on the hapless straggler.

"Now that was a rush," he said while pulling garden shears from the dismembered corpse's neck. An arterial spray of blood hit the ceiling while Left-Nut giggled like a frog-stomping schoolboy. "Money shot."

They exited the building and split up, with Left-Nut, Bruce, and Russ hauling the spoils home while the others made their way to the shuttered Halloween Store. Weeks of wearing the same clothes had left them badly needing a wardrobe change, and even cheesy costumes would be an improvement.

Russ crowbarred the door open, but they hesitated to enter. Trent articulated why. "It's blacker than Shaq's butthole in there, I'm not going first."

Charlie clicked his flashlight on and boldly led the way. Closed at the time of the outbreak, the place was decorated with fake webs and leering displays, ready for a Halloween rush that would never arrive. Even more ominous was the idea that real monsters could be lurking nearby, and every pirate, mummy and alien looked ready to pounce in the dim glow of the flashlight.

Charlie picked a cowboy outfit for himself and a Thor costume for Rob while Mike quietly snuck a French maid getup into the sack. Meanwhile, Trent searched for the kids' aisle and found himself alone in the dark, wondering if he'd heard footsteps nearby. The hair rose on the back of his neck and he got the distinct feeling that something evil was nearby. Noticing a figure in his peripheral, Trent turned and swung his sledgehammer with a startled fury, striking something and falling down in the process. A decapitated mannequin tumbled onto Trent and sent him further into a frenzy. He tossed the dummy and limped back to the others, hyperventilating and swearing at the same time. "This place is giving me the creeps. You'll have to get Blake's Pamprin without me. I'm out."

"Okay," Mike said as he saw fear was causing the old Trent to peek out from whatever hidey-hole he'd been in. "I'll help carry the clothes home and you two can get the insulin next door." Mike looked back to Charlie as he left. "Don't worry, I'll keep the ladder ready."

"Damned right you will," Charlie said. "And nice outfit," he added with a wink.

Minutes later, Rob and Charlie pried the vet clinic open and found a heartbreaking scene. Countless dogs, cats, and the occasional rabbit had died in their cages, literally left to rot. Some had struggled to break free by gnawing at the bars until their teeth gave out. The tragedy was too much for Rob to process and he took his helmet off and slumped to the ground.

Ignoring his friend rocking back and forth like a child, Charlie found several lifesaving vials in the fridge and a box of penicillin for himself. He turned to Rob. "Come on, buddy." Just then, a faint scratching noise could be heard.

"What was that?" Rob said.

"Don't know, don't care. Let's go." Charlie made his way to the door.

Rob ignored him and frantically searched the cages for any possible survivors. He had almost given up when a faint movement in a trashcan caught his eye. Rob carefully pulled a tiny ball of fur out and held it up to the flashlight. Satisfied, they hustled across the street and up the ladder.

"Check it out," Rob said. "We got the medicine and I found a kitten. Only bummer is I think it was born without eyes." He put the little thing down on the coffee table.

Smokey pet it. "He's cute. What are you gonna name him?"

Rob smiled. "What else? Elvis."

Mike examined the squirming critter and fought back a belly laugh. "That not a kitten, it's a baby raccoon."

"You dumbass," Left-Nut said and quickly backed out of swatting range.

"What was it doing in the clinic?" Bruce said.

Mike examined the raccoon as it made weird cooing and clicking noises. "Its momma might have left it there to forage and never came back. My bet would be one of those big-ass rats got to it. Nasty critters."

"What about its eyes?" Rob asked with fear in his voice.

"It hasn't opened them yet," Mike said. "But it looks healthy otherwise."

Rob breathed a heavy sigh of relief. "We can keep it?"

"I don't see why not, but you'll need to get powdered formula and parasite medicine from the clinic." Mike flipped the raccoon over. "And you need to pick out a new name. This little guy's a girl." Rob looked uncomfortable with the last bit of news, and Mike relented. "Fine then, Elvis it is. But remember, like a baby, you need to feed her every three hours."

Rob sniffled, paused, and began sobbing again. "I never had a pet before." In a nice surprise, Brandon hesitantly stroked Elvis and beamed a gap-toothed smile.

"I'll get a box and some towels so we can make her a bed," Charlie said.

Still unable to speak, Rob followed him into the kitchen.

Not everyone was excited about their new roommate, however. "That's great. First an orphan and now a rodent. Next I suppose we'll be housing bedbugs and carnies," Left-Nut said. "And I'm not cleaning up any shit."

"You know, that raccoon already has more friends here than you do," Blake said ruefully while grabbing his medicine. He turned to Mike after inspecting one of the cloudy vials. "Is it supposed to look like this? The stuff I use looks like water."

Mike took the container, shook it vigorously, and handed it back. "This is made for dogs and it wasn't refrigerated either, but it's all we have. It's your call if you want to take it or not. I guess it depends on how you're feeling."

"Like shit."

Mike rested his hand on Blake's shoulder. "Then there's your answer."

Blake nodded grimly and then jabbed the syringe into his arm with a wince. "Good thing I was born lucky."

Chapter 30
Mama Said Knock You Out

The locker room shook from blaring speakers and the stomping of ten thousand fans. After paying a seventy-dollar admission, drinking eight-dollar draft Pabst Blue Ribbons and having exhausted their stories about how much ass they kicked in high school, the sold out Vegas crowd grew anxious for the main event. It was like updating the Roman Coliseum with crystal meth and hard-on prescriptions. This was the big time, and Big Rob prepared for the fight as he always did.

Blaaaaugh. Two chili dogs, a peanut-butter milkshake, twelve crab rangoons and a meat-lovers pizza sprayed the sink in a frothy eruption. The stench was enough to make one question the very existence of God.

"Jesus that's foul," Charlie said while covering his nose. "Looks like you haven't stuck to your diet. Is that a whole head of garlic?" It was.

Tremors rocked the giant's body as he lost control again and Charlie jumped to avoid a direct whiff of the nastiness. The inexperienced trainer stared at the hodgepodge no sane man would eat just three hours before a nationally televised fight.

"It's only nerves, I'll be fine," Rob said unconvincingly.

"Good thing you're too cheap to pay me because I'd be mad as hell right now. I mean, you're walking into a meat grinder stuffed like a suckling pig." Charlie paused as another pungent smell assaulted his senses — Rob's body odor. "When's the last time you showered? You smell like ass dipped in cabbage."

Rob wiped the slime from his beard and then splashed water on his ghostly white face. He peered into the mirror. "How do I look?"

"Like you've been eaten by a wolf and shit off a cliff... so pretty much like normal." He slapped his friend on the back and smiled a toothy grin. "Now stop being a pussy and get your head on straight. You've got a belt to win. Think about it, this could set you up for life."

Rob's steely blue eyes sparkled as he imagined what might be if he could only pull off the unthinkable. "It would be nice to have extra cash. I'll be able to pay rent on time, maybe pick up some sponsors. I might even get to upgrade from nailing fat chicks to ugly chicks."

"Aiming high indeed. So... not to put any more pressure on you, but..." Charlie dropped his humorous tone and stared deeply at his friend. "Look, I maxed out my credit cards and put ten grand down. Boom goes the dynamite."

"Why did you do that?"

"Because I know you can do it. We've got thirty to one odds right now. This is our big break. Beat this guy's ass and there's no looking back for both of us. 2003 is the year we come out on top."

Rob's eyes glistened. "Thanks for believing in me."

Charlie was the only person that did. Rob's mother had died years earlier from treatable cancer and his abusive father skipped town after a teenaged Rob gave him a massive beat down. The last time he saw his dad was on the show *To Catch a Predator*.

Charlie's family took the lovable loser in, treated him as one of their own and eventually got him into college on a wrestling scholarship. After five years of grade inflation and plenty of charity, he graduated with a worthless P.E. degree and no job prospects. Two years later, Rob was penniless and living in a tent, but still struggling for a shot at greatness.

And Charlie had one foot in the gutter right along with him. Fired from his teaching job months earlier for missing work and getting wasted at the office Christmas party, this could be either Charlie's major rebound or his last spiral around the toilet.

"You can blow me later. Now get your gloves on and kick that Euro-trash's dick in the dirt." It wasn't a bad pep talk considering he'd downed four Jager-Bombs and snorted two lines of coke. Charlie was a little nervous too, after all.

"Fuck yeah!" Rob punched a locker with enthusiasm and crumpled it like a pop can.

Unfortunately, his opponent was the much-favored reigning MMA World Champion, Vladimir Draganov. Bulgaria's favorite bad boy was a judo expert and an amateur rapist. Known for his roundhouse knockouts and million-dollar sexual assault payoffs, Vladimir would be near impossible to beat. The promoters had even hand-picked Rob to be the sacrificial tomato can and banked on a highlight-reel whipping.

But Rob and Charlie held the wildcards of stupidity and desperation firmly in their grasp, and they were ready to toss them on the table. To be sure, Vladimir outclassed Rob when it came to technical skills, training, and of course, nutrition. Rob had a puncher's chance though, and that's what Charlie was counting on. He'd personally seen Rob own three guys at a keg party without putting down his hot dog, literally taking a bite between knockouts. The behemoth had powerful arms, hammer-like fists, and a tree trunk of a neck.

Now suited up and ready for combat, the duo walked down a winding hallway and stopped at the entrance to the arena, waiting for the announcer's call. The sound of the crowd was deafening.

"And now, the challenger, fighting out of Stormburg, Illinois... with a mixed martial arts record of ten wins and zero losses, standing at a full six-foot eight inches and weighing in at a massive two-hundred and ninety pounds... The Titan of the Midwest... Viking Rob Magnusson!" Fireworks erupted as Rob stepped into the aisle bathed in multi-colored spotlights. He raised his meaty arms and waited for a song by 80's metal band Slayer. But the heavy tune "Seasons of the Abyss" never kicked on. What did play over the massive sound system was a song popular at countless wedding receptions and bar mitzvahs the world over — a little ditty called "The Chicken Dance."

Panic gripped Rob as he turned to Charlie. "What the fuck? I didn't pick this shit."

Charlie shoved him back towards the ring and shouted above the blaring noise, "I have no idea, dude, just go with it." The crowd raucously clapped to the beat as the two bumbling friends appeared on the jumbo screen and on millions of televisions across the country. A thousand miles away, Left-Nut rolled on the floor in an uncontrollable fit of laughter. This was the happiest moment of his life.

Rob slunk towards the dressing room as beer cans whizzed past his head, and Charlie tried to stop him. After much coaxing, a deflated Rob turned and stiffly made his way to the ring.

The soundboard operator responsible for the "mix up" smiled broadly in the control room, knowing the five grand in cash he'd gotten from Vladimir would keep him knee deep in Oxycontin and Filipino hookers for quite some time. In Vegas, a person never knew when a jackpot was right around the corner.

Thankfully, the song ended as the two men reached the metal cage amid flashbulbs and jeers. Charlie searched his mind for any last minute advice. "Get inside and use your weight. You need to wear him out fast, so lean on him every chance you get. When he tires, hug him and go for a deep clinch, then take him down and pound his face into jelly." Rob's attention continued to wander, so Charlie grabbed him roughly by the jaw and gave him a smack. "Focus, man, focus."

Rob snapped out of the panic spiral. "I got this."

"Welcome back. If you give him any room to breathe, he'll knock your ass out. So what you gotta do is—"

The announcer started up again. "And now... fighting out of Tryavna, Bulgaria, with the astounding mixed martial arts record of twenty wins, sixteen by knockout...

with two losses by disqualification... standing six foot four and weighing in at two hundred and forty pounds... holder of three world heavyweight belts... known the world over as the Bulgarian Badass... the champion... Vladimir, The Dragon, Draganov!"

Fireworks exploded in an orgy of smoke and clatter as the champ slowly descended to LL Cool J's "Mama Said Knock You Out." Dancing the entire time, it took him five minutes to reach the ring. Big Rob looked shell-shocked once again and it was clear the shenanigans had paid off.

The music stopped and Charlie popped Rob's mouthpiece into place. "Knuckles up, brother, I'll see you soon." As the words left his mouth, Charlie wondered if he was lying. He didn't like his own answer.

Big Rob shuffled to the center of the ring and came face to face with the cauliflower-eared champ. Vladimir spoke as the ref had them tap gloves. "Try not lay egg, big chicken."

The Bulgarian's words were jumbled, but Rob realized Vladimir had embarrassed him in front of the world with his little song stunt. The taunt was the final insult, and Rob fixed his opponent with a red-hot glare and prepared to let his fists do the talking.

Charlie didn't hear Vladimir, but he did see Rob's reaction. He'd been the butt of jokes his entire life and usually turned the other cheek. Now all that suppressed rage bubbled up to the surface like a force of nature. Rob stood taller. His eyes, once shifting and distracted, now focused like a laser on Vladimir.

"Shit's about to go thunder-dome!" Charlie yelled and banged on the cage.

The bell rang and Rob charged forward like an enraged bull. But the matador answered with a quick combination of crisp jabs and tried to follow with a fight-ending upper-cut. Rob simply absorbed the blows and pressed forward, deflecting the haymaker and taking the champ down.

Ten thousand fans gasped in unison as the Bulgarian Badass landed hard on his back. Quick as a spider, Rob moved into a full guard position while Charlie shouted,

"Ground and pound, ground and pound!" He'd never seen Rob move with such glorious purpose.

Meanwhile, Vladimir wondered how he'd ended up on his back fifteen seconds into the fight, and was surprised at the ferocity of the charge. Still, the veteran had been in tighter spots than this and choked out opponents from that very position. He simply needed to cover up until his eager opponent made a mistake, and they always did. However, that confidence vanished after three powerful hammer strikes slipped past his defenses and shattered his nose. The punches continued one after another like pistons in an engine, and Vladimir ate most of them.

Rob's blows quickly lost their mustard as the adrenaline faded and he began to gas out. He leaned forward to let his stench take over.

A battered and bloody Vladimir struggled to breathe as the garlicky essence seeped out of Rob's sweaty pores. He couldn't breathe, and a man known for putting women in painful positions now found himself in one. The coward slowly made a move to tap out.

Meanwhile, the shady owner of the fight league was not enjoying the show. "I can't have that lard-ass be the face of my empire," he said through puffs of a Cuban cigar. "This ain't happening." He made a call to the referee's pager.

Getting his signal, the ref jumped in. "Okay, no resting on top. I'm standing you up for inactivity." Of course, it was crap, and the fans went ballistic. Though drunken and ignorant, they still wanted to see a fair fight and this professional wrestling bullshit would not do.

Vladimir's panic ebbed as he got back to his feet, and his superior skills kicked in. He circled to the right while peppering the plucky upstart with jab after jab. A nasty cut opened over Rob's left eye and obscured his vision. Twenty long seconds remained in the first round. Ten... five... Another jab followed by a crushing right hook to Rob's jaw. Three... two... one... *Ding*.

Both fighters staggered to their corners looking like they'd walked through a gauntlet. Vladimir had the best men money could buy and Rob had... Charlie. The champ's crew smeared Vaseline over cuts and applied cold metal to a nasty forehead welt. Charlie, however, leered at the ring girl bent over in front of him. The knockout picked up her sign and cast him a come-hither look.

"Water," Rob managed to gasp out, and the rookie trainer turned from the floozy and instinctively squirted a stream down the fighter's chasm of a mouth. Distracted by the perfect body before him, Charlie forgot to remove Rob's mouth guard. The ice-cold water bounced off the plastic and traveled directly into Rob's over-taxed lungs. It was a huge blunder, and Rob was still hacking up water when the bell rang.

Vladimir, however, had regained his wind as well as his confidence. A cold smile crossed his battered face upon seeing Rob's condition.

"Get your hands up!" Charlie said and banged on the cage as the fight, and his livelihood, started slipping away.

Rob feebly raised his fists into a half-assed defensive posture as Vladimir closed in rapidly. A flurry of head-strikes followed by a powerful sidekick to his gut sent shockwaves through Rob's entire body. He wobbled for a moment and his hands dropped just a few inches.

It was the opening the champ needed, and he spun into his signature roundhouse kick. Rob tried to back away, but the blow landed squarely on his thick jaw. The giant tipped backwards like a felled sequoia and landed with a thunderous boom as the crowd went absolutely ape-shit. This was what they had paid for.

The referee dashed to Rob's side and motioned for the ringside doctors, leaving a shell-shocked Charlie alone and decimated. Worrying about his friend's health, Charlie also wondered how they would even get back to Illinois.

Meanwhile, Vladimir bounced around doing the chicken dance and acting like his regular jagoff self. That's when the Bulgarian Badass stopped his theatrics and pointed to Rob's motionless form as the doctors applied a neck brace. The television camera zoomed in on a rapidly enlarging golden puddle that was forming in the center of the ring. Hello *YouTube*, goodbye fighting career.

*   *   *

Lathered in sweat, Big Rob Magnusson woke from his recurring flashback-nightmare. "Dang." The couch beneath him was soaked. He crept to the window and tossed his soiled underwear into the road, where it landed next to the charred mound that was Blake's funeral pyre.

Though a month had passed since Blake died from the spoiled insulin, his last words still echoed in Rob's mind. "I swear you could fuck up a peanut butter sandwich." Rob put on his tattered jean shorts, flipped the cushion over and lay back down to sleep.

Chapter 31
Booty Call

A casualty of the Second Great Chicago Fire, Willis Tower had collapsed upon itself and blanketed the city in a fine layer of dust and despair. Like its residents, America's Second City had died.

However, Charlie Campbell's thoughts were elsewhere as he snuck about the shadows, kicking up a powdery trail between burnt out cars and overgrown bushes. And they were mostly on getting laid.

While his friends continued their idle boozing and general mischief-making, Charlie pounded out countless pushups, sit-ups and wind sprints. The hardcore training soon re-shaped him into the White Lightning of old, albeit balder than before, but just as fast. Now able to survive on the streets through speed and cunning, Charlie grew bolder with each solo trip. Tonight he hoped to score a secret rendezvous with the elusive neighbor girls. Naturally, he'd kept his friends in the dark about his plans.

The streets were almost empty due to Russ's invention of a game he called "zom-bowling." A bowling ball screwed to a long chain was the only equipment, and being drunk was the only rule. Anything dumb enough to get into range went splat, and the rats always cleaned up the mess. It passed the time.

After a few pauses to avoid detection, Charlie reached the three-flat apartment down the street, grabbed a knotted bed sheet hanging from the second floor window, and clamored up. Adrenaline pumping, he entered the darkened room intent on making a bold entrance. "Hello, ladies," Charlie said and offered up the broadest smile he could muster. He had always thought first impressions were important.

The answer was a sharp object pressed firmly against his neck. Blood spattered the floor as echoes of the bachelor party fiasco flooded Charlie's thoughts. He feared his dick had betrayed him yet again.

"Sit down and put your hands above your head," said a gruff female voice from the darkness.

Charlie complied. "I'm unarmed—"

"Shut your mouth," came the reply.

Charlie pressed his luck. "I risked my ass bringing you food. Plus you dropped me a note and told me to come up here. What gives?"

A hastily lit candle revealed the two women holding him captive. "We've been watching you since day one," a redhead built like a brick shithouse said as she pushed the knife forward. "And frankly, we're not impressed."

Charlie cringed. "I'm not sure what you think you've seen from a hundred yards away, but—"

"We've seen plenty," she replied, stone-faced. "I'd say we know everything about you."

"Oh really?"

"For instance, your white-haired friend is a bumbling masturbatory idiot. The moron with the mullet is a raging alcoholic, the big guy looks borderline retarded and the smirking tool in the cop outfit is a psycho. How did I do?"

"Not bad," Charlie conceded. "But what about me?"

"You seem the least useless out of the bunch," the other girl, a blonde, said with the faintest hint of a smile. Charlie saw his lifeline.

"We're not boy scouts, but we've been trying. Don't we get points for rescuing the kid at least?"

"Saving him was the only reason we contacted you," the blonde said.

"You just used us for food then?"

She shook her head. "No. We wanted to make sure you were harmless."

"And?" Charlie asked.

"And I'm pretty sure Kate here could kick your ass," she replied with a wink.

Charlie glanced sideways at his captor's taut arms. "Fair enough. So that's Kate. I'm Charlie, what's your name?"

Her face softened. "Brooke."

"Nice to meet you. Now that we're old friends, would you mind taking the knife out of my neck? I don't want to bleed out over here."

Kate lowered the blade and stepped away. "You're both annoying the shit outta me so I'm going to the living room. Don't make me come back in here, pencil neck."

"Sorry, she doesn't like men... at all," Brooke whispered while leaning in and dabbing at Blake's puncture wound with a rag.

"I kinda got that feeling," he said through gritted teeth. "What about you? Because I might actually be the world's most eligible bachelor."

"Being a little forward aren't you?" she said while her green eyes sparkled.

Charlie nodded. "There's no reason not to be, given the circumstances. I mean, I could die on my way home."

"Merlot?" she asked casually and retrieved a bottle from the counter. "I've been saving it."

"Tempting, but I stopped drinking a few weeks ago and I'm kinda on a roll. But if you wanna get hammered and do something you'll regret..."

The banter kept up for several hours and Charlie was on top of his game. It felt great, but the sun was coming up soon and he had to sneak home.

"I almost forgot," Charlie said and gave her a freshly picked red rose from Mrs. Stone's beloved garden, plucked mere feet from the heavily decayed and thoroughly crushed skeleton. "Are we going steady now?"

"I'm not that easy," she said and smiled. "Then again, you are quite eligible."

"But all bullshit aside, why am I here?"

Brooke put down her empty glass. "We want to leave the city, and we need your help to do it."

Chapter 32
You Mad Bro?

"This bar was great. They'd give you free drinks and food all night long," Rob said then paused from his story to gulp stale rum and coke. "When it got late, they'd take you out back and fuck the shit out of you."

"This actually happened to you?" Bruce said.

"No, but it happened to my sister all the time."

Charlie moved on before any feelings or faces could get hurt. "I can't believe how much Elvis and Brandon are growing," he said as the dynamic duo happily splashed around the kiddie pool, shaded from the sun by a Bud Light umbrella. The raccoon and child had become the best of friends, almost like brothers.

"They're growing all right. Like a cancer," sourpuss Left-Nut added.

"What's up your ass?" Charlie said. "Not that I really give two shits."

"All right, since you asked me. I'm sick of you walking around here like you're Jesus, and all of us should just bow down to your greatness. The truth of the matter is, you're the biggest traitor since Mariah Stevens—"

"Who's that?" Russ paused from meticulously brushing his mullet. Five hundred strokes a day like clockwork.

"My prom date," Left-Nut replied. "I went for snacks and that whore gave my cousin a handy-j under the table. But she's not important. What's important is that we've got our own Benedict Arnold, right in front of us."

"Oh here we go. I suppose you're gonna say I stole your jerk-off lotion or something?"

Left-Nut stopped inches from Charlie's face. "Oh no, this is legit." He turned back to the others. "I noticed our food stocks were shrinking. Of course, I assumed Rob was stealing it, being the fat fuck that he is, so I waited to catch him in the act. It took a few nights of staying up late, pretending I was asleep on the couch." He whirled around dramatically to face Charlie. "Only the thief wasn't Rob."

"I've been carbo-loading, big deal. I bring most of the food in anyways."

Left-Nut sneered. "If it were only that simple. But I was curious to see what you were up to, so I tailed you one night. And that's when I saw you climb into a three-flat down the block, your dick leading the way."

"Where are you goin' with this?"

"I'm saying I want my piece, literally. Besides, I called dibs on the blonde one. That's official."

"Don't you think she has a say about that?" Charlie said as his face reddened and blood rushed to his hands.

"There's no free lunch. If they want more food, they'll have to pay. Ass, gas or grass right? I know what I'll take."

Mike jumped in. "You're a rapist now?"

"Haven't you been paying attention for the last fifteen years?" Left-Nut's voice rose. "You could say that I have questionable morals, sure."

Mike nodded. "You could say that."

Left-Nut stood his ground. "Here we go again. Mike thinks his shit doesn't stink too. But I remember back in college you stuck your roommate's toothbrush up your ass because he stole your beer."

"Hey, I was Mike's roommate," Smokey said, surprised.

"It's called growing up. Most people that aren't complete losers tend to do it." Mike looked to Smokey. "Sorry about the toothbrush. I guess I overacted a little."

The arguments continued while Brandon and Elvis romped in the rainwater, blissfully unaware of the drama unfolding around them. Brandon had learned to mimic the raccoon's chatter and now it was the only noise he would make, much to Left-Nut's annoyance.

Meanwhile, the dispute picked up steam as others took sides. "I don't normally agree with Lefty, but he's got a point," Bruce said. "I'm not risking my life for chicks I've never even met. Especially when Charlie's getting all the honey. That's bogus."

"It's worse than bogus," Trent said. "It's damn right dangerous. I mean, Charlie's been going out without telling any of us?"

"Yeah, so? I don't have a curfew."

"You haven't had a bite check, which means you could be infected right now and we wouldn't even know it," Trent replied. "We don't want another Cliff situation on our hands. Better tie him up until we figure this out."

"Yeah, then we can pay our neighbors a house call," Left-Nut added with a knowing smirk. "And by house call I mean sexual intercourse."

The last comment sent ice through Charlie's veins and spurred him to act. He braced for the quick shove that would send Left-Nut tumbling down into the zombie-pit. The others were drunk enough that they might back off, and if not, well, he'd deal with them too. Things were about to get real.

"What's that noise?" Rob said while positioning himself between Charlie and the others. "Seriously, everybody shut up for second."

"Like the helicopter you 'heard' the other day?" Russ said. "Boy, I swear you got oatmeal between your ears."

"Not another word," Big Rob replied with a glare, and Russ went back to sipping his grain alcohol.

Sure enough, a low rumble grew louder, and the guys instantly forgot their squabble. That's when the building began rattling.

Bruce ran to the north side of the roof and leaned far over the edge, right in time to see a tank come around the corner and turn down their street, mowing down several zombies in the process. "Over here!" he shouted and waved frantically. A machine gunner wearing sunglasses gestured back as the tan-colored tank came closer.

"Holy shit, here comes the cavalry!" Bruce squinted when he noticed the tank bore a red flag with yellow stars. "What's a Chinese tank doing—"

CHAH CHAH CHAH CHAH CHAH! was the sound of the .50 caliber ripping the stockbroker in half. Bruce's legs stood upright, almost cartoon-like, as his limp torso splashed into the crimson pool.

Russ instinctively chucked his bottle of liquor at the tank, then dove for cover as the gunner sprayed more belt-fed shells in his direction. The incoming firepower easily shredded the brick façade of the building and sent shards flying into the handful of idiots now facing certain death.

"Where's my bullets?" Trent said while cowering behind the gas grill.

"You're serious?" Charlie replied. "It's a fucking tank."

"You got a better idea?"

He didn't. "They're in Jim's bible."

Naturally, this was the only place that Trent hadn't searched. Moments later, he returned with his gun and remaining ammo. The cop waited for a break in the firing, then popped up and squeezed off several rounds at the soldier, completely missing him. With the machine gun now trained directly at him, he fired his last round and missed again, but this time the bullet ricocheted off the tank and caused a spark. Russ's liquor and the gunner went up in flames.

As the gunplay and death scream of the flaming soldier radiated outward, hordes of zombies flooded in from surrounding areas and swarmed onto the tank, some catching fire in their mad rush to consume the living. But the turret turned and rose towards the apartment, threatening to obliterate the friends with the push of a button. Out of ammo, Trent yelled a string of Asian-based obscenities as he grabbed his crotch with one hand and threw his pistol with the other.

BOOM! The tank promptly exploded, shattering every window on the block and shaking the foundation of the apartment to its core.

In the commotion, no one had noticed the Black Hawk helicopter swoop down and unload hell. It was the good guys this time.

"I knew I heard a chopper," Rob said as he rose from shielding Brandon, ignoring the piece of sizzling shrapnel sticking from his back.

The next few minutes were a mad scramble to deal with the small fires spreading throughout the building. As gruesome as it was, buckets of bloody Bruce-water was the only way to get it done. While they put out the last of the flames, Rob noticed someone was missing. "Where's Elvis?" he said with panic creeping into his voice.

A quick search revealed nothing until Brandon pointed across the street. The raccoon was at ground level, weaving his way past burning debris and shambling zombies with a dozen giant rats in hot pursuit. Rob went berserk, and it took everyone to restrain him as a screeching Elvis fled down an alley.

But they couldn't dwell on the raccoon's fate for too long because a sudden downwash told them the helicopter had returned. With the wind whipping his hair, Russ shouted upwards, "Drop a ladder! Get me the fuck out of here!" The reply was a large rock striking Russ in the forehead and knocking him out cold.

Mike un-crumpled a note taped to the rock and read it aloud. "Area too hot. Meet at park three blocks north. Sunrise, two weeks from today. Last ride out."

The helicopter flew off as abruptly as it had arrived, leaving behind thousands of extra zombies drawn by its presence — zombies now blocking their new escape route.

Searching for his inner John Wayne, Charlie addressed his battered friends. "Time to get to work, boys."

Chapter 33
Spring Flower

Sergeant Zhang removed his bloody helmet and wiped the sweat from his brow with a camouflaged handkerchief. The stocky class-two sergeant of the People's Liberation Army concentrated on a map for the fifth time. The long monsoons of Liaoning Province made Chicago summers pale in comparison, so it wasn't the heat throwing him off. No, what rattled Zhang was the overwhelming stench of rotting corpses and the non-stop pace of battle.

The old man understood well the ugliness of war. Firing on civilians at Tiananmen Square long ago and storming the beaches of Taiwan more recently had prepared him for that. But nothing could prime him for the carnage of the North American theatre.

Of the twenty thousand troops from Zhang's division, the pride of Shenyang Military Region, under five thousand remained. Since a disastrous border crossing from Canada, they'd been bombed, strafed, sniped and even eaten until only a scant handful survived from his original squad. Still, the sergeant knew China could afford losses like that. It was all part of the plan after all.

Lack of sleep was pushing him closer to madness by the hour, and he trusted no one. A soldier that failed to look him in the eye would earn a swift rifle butt to the head, and any type of insubordination meant summary execution. These "morale boosters" had brought many of his men to their breaking point.

Most recently, Sergeant Zhang's squad moved to section eight-C, also known as Wicker Park, for a clean sweep and holding action. The orders were simple, neutralize any Americans, infected or not, and then secure the area. Artillery, tanks, heavy machine guns and flamethrowers had created a gory, yet highly choreographed, invasion of the city. Resistance was rapidly shrinking, but only from the living.

In theory, the Chinese population was supposed to be immune to the pandemic virus, but this wasn't always the case. That uncertainty led to a strict policy of shooting compromised soldiers, and that was happening plenty as they pushed into the more populated areas. The latest example was a former schoolteacher with a lovely singing voice by the name of Wu Ming. He went out singing an ode to Chairman Mao and brought many to tears.

It was the first time Zhang regretted his no exceptions policy, but there had been little choice. One infection could spiral out of control and destroy a whole unit in minutes. He'd seen it happen up close, only escaping by hiding in an abandoned refrigerator.

Zhang clapped his hands to gather the troops for another mission. "I've learned one of our 62's recently broke off communications in section ten-B, just north of here. We have been tasked with sending scouts to locate the tank." This was a bullshit mission and Zhang knew it. A two-mile trip into no-man's land was almost certain suicide, and that's why he planned to use several of his weakest links in the operation.

Twenty-three year old Yi Chen faked a pleasant smile while hiding the terror that clawed at his stomach like a parasite. *Don't pick me, don't pick me, don't pick me.* He held his breath as the sergeant studied a crumpled up piece of paper.

"I have chosen for this honorable mission Private Lin, Private Wu, Private Cai and Private *Duànbèi.*" There were a few chuckles at the mention of the last name.

Yi Chen's heart sank. On top of being chosen, Zhang had called him "Private Duànbèi." Private Brokeback. Apparently, winning a bronze medal after landing a flawless

Yamashita style vault in the World Games wasn't enough to earn respect among this group. Chen no longer heard the orders as blood pumped in his head faster and faster.

"Make visual contact with the tank, note its location, assess its condition and radio your findings directly to me. Your secondary mission is to locate the crew by checking the surrounding area. Duànbèi, are you listening?"

Chen snapped back into the moment and answered fast enough to avoid a vicious thrashing. "Yes, sir. It will be an honor to carry out this mission. I will not let you down."

"You have five minutes to pack and head out. Anyone have questions?" Dead silence greeted him as usual. Having questions often turned to having beatings. "Good." Finished, Sergeant Zhang returned to the shade of a burned out tanning salon to finish drinking something they'd found called Mountain Dew. It was giving him quite a buzz.

Yi Chen donned his pack and checked his automatic rifle for problems. The QBZ-95 had seen plenty of action lately, almost becoming an extension of his own powerfully built body. Even the bayonet had saved his life in close combat with the infected, and Chen made sure it was razor sharp.

Finally, he prayed to his elders. During the quiet contemplation, Chen sought wisdom and courage to maintain his secret oath. He would avoid harming the innocent at all costs. His "poor" aim had earned him the scorn of fellow soldiers but helped keep his conscience clean, and that was important enough for Chen to risk his own life.

Private Wu, a lean and foul-tempered man, snuck up on Chen and sent him sprawling to the ground with a forceful kick to the rear. "Hurry up, Liúmáng. We don't have time for your fantasies about cock-gobbling boyfriends." Wu snorted loudly after calling Chen a pervert and looked to his comrades for approval. But most simply kept quiet, not wanting to ridicule a condemned man. Besides, they figured Wu wouldn't be coming back either.

Chen ignored the man he could snap in half like a dry twig and finished his thoughts. The kind-hearted soldier never bothered explaining how he'd actually been happily married. Chen wouldn't sully the image of his wife, the beautiful Chunhua, by even mentioning her in his current company of scoundrels.

She was Chen's "Spring Flower," and her memory would remain his and his alone. His wife had been gone for several years now, but he still thought about her almost every waking moment, and took any chance he could to remember the sound of her voice. The memory of her face however, slipped further and further away from him with each day.

The government had promised to provide for everyone during the Great Famine, but Chunhua's village had been passed over so party leaders could feed their own families. When Chen finally earned leave after two years of fierce service, all he found waiting was an empty house and a shallow grave. The gymnast never even learned who buried her. But after the betrayal, Chen swore an oath to remain faithful to the memory of his Spring Flower, and he would gladly die to honor it. He believed he would soon get that chance.

Chapter 34
The Windy City

What remained of Bruce had been tossed into the street with little fanfare. The place was too thick with zombies for a burial now, not to mention the new threat of a mecha-nized Chinese army. Russ summed up their predicament while puffing a menthol cigarette. "We're boned."

"It's another hurdle," Mike said unconvincingly. "We'll have to be more careful but it doesn't change our goals, just how we get to them."

"Look, you can't make chicken salad out of chicken shit," Russ said. "Face it, if the zombies don't get us, the god-damned communists will. Fuck it, I'm gonna get drunk."

"You'd have to sober up first," Charlie said. "But Mike's right. We'll start clearing the streets now. I've got some ideas that might work." His plan to help the women escape had grown in complexity and danger, but the prospect of a chopper ride to safety would be well worth the risk. "And Left-Nut, say another word about those girls and I turn you into a wind chime."

"What in the shit are the Chinese doing here anyways?" Smokey said.

"No clue, but I bet they'll come looking for their tank," Charlie replied. "Which means we need to get moving." The men agreed and started culling the massive zombie herd while Charlie and Mike spitballed the specifics of a new escape plan.

Trent fired his Everclear loaded Super-Soaker into the mass of staggering cannibals below while Smokey chucked a lit roll of toilet paper into the mix. The blazing figures ran around like stuntmen before collapsing into piles of smoldering tinder while Russ enjoyed the show.

"Tell me what you got," Mike said as the stench and smoke overtook them.

"God, that reeks. Anyways, that morning I'll sneak the girls over and we'll use the ladder to go from rooftop to rooftop until we reach the end of the block. We'll need to practice a few times and secure the route to make sure there aren't surprises along the way. We time the stereo to go off and draw any stragglers back to our apartment, then we drop down and sprint to the finish line."

"You just thought of this?" Mike asked.

"Actually, I've been planning to leave for a while now, but you probably knew that." As the two conversed, Rob began using a painter's pole with a steak knife taped to the end as a spear. Smokey dangled over the side as bait while Rob gigged the stragglers like frogs. The streets were clear after several hours of the gruesome work and the men went down to inspect the ruined tank.

Somehow, the machine gun was still intact and after several minutes of shit-talking and finger pointing, they were able to detach and carry it to the roof along with boxes of unexploded ammo. Having the heavy gun would give them a much needed confidence boost, and everyone wanted the chance to fire it off when the time was right.

Mike and Charlie started practicing the building hopping technique as the sun set. It worked by extending the thirty foot ladder straight into the air and then lowering one end to the roof of the next building. Next, they'd cross the rickety pseudo-bridge, rinse and repeat.

"I wish we had thought of this before," Mike said as he padlocked the roof access door of the last building on their escape route.

"Yeah, it's the only way to travel." Charlie shivered as he noticed a sudden temperature drop. "Better head home soon. I think a storm's brewing."

The pair made their way back uneventfully as dark clouds rolled in and lightning flashed in the distance.

Storms were always welcome as they brought cooler temperatures, needed water and a chance to shower. This one had the added benefit of dousing flaming piles of corpses.

Charlie placed the ladder down and carefully crossed the rungs until he felt the familiar roof of their apartment beneath his feet. He turned as Mike followed behind. "I bet in a hurry we could make the trip in ten minutes."

"I'd say more like fifteen when you take into account... oh fuck—" A large gust of wind barreled down the alley and threw Mike off balance. His left foot fell between the rungs and he hit his crotch on the metal ladder before slipping off the side.

Charlie gasped when his friend dropped out of sight, and visions of Jim's ruined body came to mind as he ran to the edge. But Mike was on his back and waving up with a big smile plastered on his face. As luck would have it, a pile of dispatched zombies had broken his fall. "Don't stand there, drop the ladder down," he whispered.

Russ was nearby and helped Charlie position the ladder while Mike played possum. But as Mike rose to make his escape, something else rose with him. Apparently, a creature on the bottom of the pile hadn't been quite dead, and Mike's movement triggered a reflex, causing it to lash out. He shoved the wounded creature off and followed with a powerful swing of his hammer, putting the mohawked zombie down with a well-placed blow to the temple.

A nearly out of breath Mike sprang up top as his friends gathered around. "I thought you were a goner. Twice," Charlie said while giving him a bear hug.

"I think I almost shit my pants twice," Mike replied with a grin. "Literally, I almost shit my pants."

Charlie's smile disappeared as blood began trickling from Mike's nose. "Did you hit your head?" The trickle became a gush.

"No," Mike said and turned pale while pinching his nose.

Trent backed up and settled behind the machine gun. "Dude, I think you got bit. Take your shirt off so we can check. It's your rule after all."

Mike gave in, revealing a round indentation on his shoulder. "It's just a scratch from the fall."

"Bullshit," Trent said as the mark turned purple, then black before their eyes. Large raindrops began to fall from the sky.

"I can't believe it. I just..." Mike's shoulders slumped.

Charlie moved in front of Trent's line of fire. "Everybody take a deep breath. If he's infected we can put him in the alley with Cliff, and... and if there's a cure we can come back." It didn't make sense but he had to try.

Mike sighed loudly. "No thanks, I saw what these assholes did to Cliff."

"He can't stay here another minute," Trent said. His face softened. "I'm sorry, but he's a ticking time bomb."

"I understand." Mike put his shirt back on. "I'll go. Maybe being a zombie won't be so bad. Maybe you daydream all day or something. I just know I don't wanna die. That's like, too final. And I always have been experimental."

Trent gritted his teeth. "I can't let you wander off either. You'd put us all in danger, even Brandon, and you know I won't let that happen."

Internally Charlie agreed with Trent, but that route was too painful. "We've killed hundreds of zombies, one more out there won't matter. Let him go."

"I'll take Vidu's moped as far away as I can. I might even stop by the zoo to see some old friends from vet school." He clutched his tightening stomach.

Trent noticed Mike's growing discomfort. "Fine, but you need to go now."

Russ stepped forward. "I know we gave you a lot of shit, but you're a righteous dude. It's too bad you had to die a gay virgin."

"I wouldn't be so sure of that, huh, Left-Nut?" Mike managed a smile as his pain intensified. "He really liked the French maid outfit."

Left-Nut squirmed as all eyes turned to him. "Hey, I was pitching and remember, I got a medical condition which means if I don't—"

"Yeah, it's called being a flamer," Russ said and gave Mike a hug before quickly backing away. "Adios, brother."

"Thanks," Mike said. "You all need to listen to Charlie if you wanna get out alive." He gave his friend a knowing look. "Follow your gut and show these knuckleheads what a real man is."

Charlie tried to reply, but the words wouldn't come. So he ruffled Mike's hair and held the ladder as his friend descended for the last time. They waved goodbye as Mike pulled the moped upright and turned the engine on. Lightning flashed as he began the mile and a half trip to the zoo, weaving around various obstacles while ignoring the growing pain in his gut.

"Focus, you've still got some life left in you," he said as several zombies gave a half-assed chase.

Mike was amazed at how easily he travelled by scooter and wondered if they could have fled the city that way. It was idle speculation though, considering he wouldn't be returning to tell anyone. Soon enough he pulled up to the main gate of the Lincoln Park Zoo and found the area surprisingly void of any movement, zombie or otherwise. He passed the turnstile and entered his familiar stomping ground. But the happy summer days spent tending to the animals were long gone, and the zoo was in utter shambles.

Still, he hoped to hold off long enough to rescue some of his furry friends. But each exhibit brought fresh disappointment and dead animals. The zebras, kangaroos, lions and others he'd known intimately were all gone, wasted away with nobody to feed them.

As Mike rested by the primate enclosure he felt a presence behind him, and for a moment the rain stopped landing on his head. He turned to see six huge forms — Baringo giraffes to be precise — staring at him. They'd somehow gotten free and wandered the zoo foraging from tree to tree. By the look of things, the herd had just about stripped the place.

"Can I get you to follow me?" he said between wet coughs. The desperate animals timidly complied, and a minute later

Mike unlocked one of the gates by the parking lot and shooed them to freedom. The last giraffe lowered its head as if to say thanks, and then followed the others to a nearby grove of trees where they hungrily tore into the foliage.

Mike had no time to celebrate as he doubled over in pain and vomited bloody mucous onto the wet pavement. He had one last place to check and at this point would have to crawl. Mike continued on willpower alone and his knees left a red trail behind him that was quickly washed away in the downpour.

What seemed like an eternity later, he reached the bear cave he'd spent so much time in, only to find it full of zookeeper corpses and empty of bears.

"Shit," he said and rolled onto his back to stare into the sky, expecting his last vision to be the tempest responsible for his demise. Instead, he got to witness a badly injured zombie crawl on top of him. "Shit!" he said much louder this time while struggling to hold the chomping creature back. Dying or not, nobody wants to get bitten.

The thing pressed down so close he could smell its fetid breath and feel its heart racing with anticipation. With one final effort, Mike pushed as hard as he could, but his strength was gone, and the zookeeper surged forward.

It was at that point Mike learned how the zombie ended up injured in the first place. The massive brown bear known affectionately as Snickers picked the zombie up and began ripping it limb from limb. With a mighty roar, the bloodied bear stood on its hind legs in victory, then advanced towards a shivering Mike.

The twelve-hundred pound beast sniffed the air as it came in for a closer look, and then planted a massive lick on Mike's face. He'd helped raise the bear as a cub years earlier after all. Reuniting with his old friend energized Mike enough to get him to his knees one final time, and he began the crawl back to the exit while Snickers followed him like an attention-starved puppy.

It was slow going but he eventually reached the open gate. Before Mike could say goodbye though, he stopped dead in his tracks, literally, as the sickness robbed his humanity. Snickers recognized something had changed and sniffed his special friend once more.

Mike calmly stood up, no longer feeling any pain besides the growing hunger in his stomach. As he began his search for human flesh, the nine-foot beast opened its enormous mouth and chomped down on the new zombie's neck, killing it instantly.

After mourning for what it thought was its mother, Snickers the bear wandered through the gate and into the raging storm, frightened and alone once more.

Chapter 35
Deadeye

Brooke smiled as she cleaned her puke from the floor. It was an odd reaction for sure, but she had been trying to get pregnant, as selfish and crazy as it was. Women hadn't stopped being mothers throughout the countless wars and famines of history, and this scenario wouldn't be an exception. At least that's what she told herself.

But now Brooke wanted to make sure it actually was morning sickness and not mild food poisoning from her random diet of canned goods and rainwater. To do that she'd have to sneak away from her sleeping roommate and grab a pregnancy test from the nearby convenience store. Since Charlie's men had gone medieval on the zombies in the neighborhood and she hadn't even seen one in days, she hoped it would be a cakewalk.

Brooke tiptoed downstairs and unlocked the multiple locks on her front door, then grabbed the wooden softball bat wedged against the stairs. That would be coming with her.

Next, she studied the area in front of her apartment for a full minute, ready to pop back inside at a moment's notice. It was quiet, so she took a deep breath and sprinted over. There were no zombies and no stereotypical female tripping and injuring herself, nothing. Brooke walked inside without incident, but her heart still pounded as she began to rummage around the foul-smelling store.

Picked clean of anything useful by her new boyfriend and the other marauding neighbors, Brooke figured a pregnancy test should still be there amongst the trash. She just had to find it. Two minutes turned to five, five to ten, and she was about to give up. The sun was rising and her return trip would already be more dangerous because of it.

Brooke searched one last pile when movement from the corner of the room caught her attention. Before she could turn though, small hands crawled up her back and onto her shoulder. Brooke stifled a scream and fumbled for the bat until she saw her reflection in the shoplifting mirror. It was no tiny zombie resting on her, but a raccoon. A raccoon named Elvis to be precise.

"You almost gave me a heart attack, little girl," she said and stroked the ornery creature's chin. "But your friends are gonna be so happy to see you. Speaking of happy..." Brooke spotted a pregnancy test peeking out from under several boxes of condoms. "Jackpot." She squatted over the white handle and did her business, then picked it up and waited a minute before checking. One red bar. She waited a little longer. Two red bars meant Brooke had a bun in the oven.

The front door swung open and she froze in place while several men barged in, speaking a harsh-sounding foreign language. Brooke pulled up her shorts and crept into the bathroom as the moment of joy turned to one of pure terror. Once inside, she locked the door and stood back, clutching Elvis in one hand and her Louisville Slugger in the other.

*　　*　　*

Private Wu shut the door behind him and surveyed the ransacked store. "The sun's coming up, so unless we want to end up like Cai, we rest here. Finding the tank can wait."

"Sounds good," Private Lin said and fingered through a stack of nudie magazines.

Wu frowned. "Damn, I thought there would be food here. I guess it's back to pork roll with mustard potato."

"You don't like egg roll?" Lin asked and looked up from a copy of *Drunken Babysitter.*

"Of course I like fucking egg roll. Just not three weeks in a row." Wu turned to Yi Chen. "Duànbèi, make yourself useful for once and guard the door. I gotta shit."

Chen scowled as he moved behind the cash register with his assault rifle. Not that he had much firepower left. Their mission had been a total disaster, and his comrades hadn't shared Private Cai's rounds following the radio specialist's demise. As it was, Chen had three clips left, and even if they found the tank soon, with every man for himself, getting back to the unit was a pipe dream.

Wu jiggled the handle to the unisex bathroom. "Why's this locked?" Lin came over to investigate and the two raised their rifles as Wu kicked the door in. The last thing they expected to see was a flying raccoon wearing a pirate shirt, but that's what they got.

Screaming like a banshee, Brooke threw Elvis at Wu and swung at Lin as the man raised his weapon to parry the blow. The force knocked the rifle from Lin's grasp, and Brooke aimed next for the man's head. But Wu quickly tossed the raccoon off and used his own rifle to knock Brooke unconscious.

Elvis scampered away as Wu scowled and wiped his bloody forehead. "After I deal with this round-eye, we skin that rat and have a decent meal for once."

Lin grinned with anticipation as sweat formed on his greasy forehead. "A dinner date?" They both chuckled while dragging the prone woman into the middle of the store, dumping her onto a pile of paper towels.

Brooke woke up but kept quiet in order to eavesdrop. Although she didn't know their language, one of them pulled her shorts down and it was crystal clear what they were after. Brooke opened her eyes and struggled. "Please stop, I'm pregnant!"

Wu's lecherous eyes widened in glee as he recognized a word from his rudimentary English training. "Pregnant?" he said while nodding his head vigorously. "I can make pregnant! I can make pregnant!"

At this point, Chen set his weapon down and approached the trio, stone-faced as usual. He took off his belt.

"Wait your turn," Lin said with the same deviant chuckle. "Besides, I thought you were a—" The latest insult was cut short as Chen broke the teenage conscript's windpipe with a powerful chop to the throat. Lin mouthed a silent scream as he fell to the ground and suffocated amongst the garbage.

Wu reached for his rifle but tripped on the pants tangled around his ankles, and the athletic Chen was upon him. He wrapped the belt tightly around the man's neck and slammed his head into the floor repeatedly. The first blow made Wu bite his own tongue off, the second shattered his teeth, and the third broke his jaw. Unfazed, Chen pounded the soldier's skull until all that remained was an oozing mess of meat and bone fit for a butcher's block.

Chen rose and then stumbled briefly as the crazy flow of hormones subsided. He steadied himself and walked over to the blonde woman cowering on the floor.

She was obviously convinced the violent beast would take over where the others had left off, and Chen realized how he must appear, shaking with righteous fury and covered in his squad mate's blood. So he smiled sheepishly and spoke the only English words he could remember. "Pizza. Batman. New York."

Brooke sobbed, this time with relief, as she realized the soldier meant no harm. She straightened her torn clothes and threw her arms around the odd savior. "Thank you," she whispered and buried her head into his chest.

Yi Chen had no clue what the attractive woman said, but her honeyed voice sent butterflies fluttering in his stomach all the same. Her warm tears trickled down his neck and mixed with the even warmer blood of his victims. She felt soft and frail against his skin, and her trembling body reminded him what it was like to be a man. He took in a deep breath. It was the first time he'd smelled a woman in three years and the scent was intoxicating. Too intoxicating. Chen's heart had just pumped a year's worth of adrenaline and testosterone throughout his body, and the girl's complete helplessness began setting off dormant predatory instincts.

Like a character from a classic werewolf movie fighting off a deadly transformation, the champion athlete closed his eyes and reigned in the sinister thoughts. It wasn't easy. He hugged the girl again, a little too hard, and breathed in deeply once more, taking her essence in one final time before releasing his grasp.

Next, Chen retrieved a sidearm from one of the bodies and placed it in the palm of her hand. *"Gāi zǒu le,"* he said, telling her to leave and pointing to the door.

Brooke nodded goodbye and sprinted outside, leaving Elvis behind in her rush to escape. An instant later, the pregnant woman was back in the safety of her apartment, nursing a bruised forehead and a damaged psyche, but otherwise fine.

Chen smiled as he watched her disappear from his sight forever, knowing he'd proven himself once more to the memory of his beloved wife. Left alone in no man's land, he realized he could be joining her at any moment. However, that wasn't his plan, so Chen loaded up on ammo, left bite marks on the dead in order to cover his crime, and picked up the search for the missing tank. He found it thirty seconds later.

The burned out hull was literally around the corner. If they'd made one more turn, his squad mates would still be alive. Not that Chen cared.

He gave a quick inspection of the tank and turned to leave when a flash of color caught his eye. Inexplicably, in the midst of all this death and destruction, a single flower grew from a pile of dirt in the middle of the road. It was so out of place, so utterly impossible, and yet, so beautiful. It had to be a sign from Chunhua. With tears forming in his eyes, the reluctant warrior knelt to smell the rose and focused his thoughts on happier times.

*   *   *

Charlie manned the heavy machine gun the moment he saw the Chinese soldier approach. He waited patiently for more troops to come into the kill zone, but none did, and it seemed the man was alone. Oddly enough, the soldier stopped and smelled the flower they'd planted in Blake's memory, and Charlie lined up his shot. Something felt wrong about it though, and so he hesitated. This was a human being, not a zombie.

The feeling soon passed and Charlie pulled the trigger, riddling the man with .50 caliber rounds. It was not as satisfying as he had expected.

Chapter 36
The Blindside

"**Y**ou're saying the dog won't make it without getting medicine?" Marquell asked the prison doctor.

"That's right. With all of the vomiting, Toby is going to need subcutaneous water treatment, anti-nausea medicine and antibiotics. Pancreatitis is a very serious condition."

Heather's voice trembled. "I told you those idiots brought back the wrong food, and now my dog's going to die?"

Marquell was not about to disappoint her again. "He'll be fine. I'll get the stuff myself, you'll see."

Heather scoffed. "Great."

"You don't want me to go?"

She sighed and put her hand on Marquell's broad chest, changing her tone. "I'm sorry. That's very big of you, Marky. This would mean a lot to me."

"It's settled then. Doc, you're coming with so we get the right stuff. Fausto, go round up the twenty hardest mother-fuckers here and get 'em suited up. We leave in an hour."

Exactly one hour later, Marquell met Heather at the main gate for a proper sendoff. "I'll be back quick, baby-girl. You're in charge and my man Fausto will do anything you tell him to while I'm gone."

Heather hugged the man responsible for the death of her husband. "Be careful, but hurry."

Full of confidence, Marquell boarded the prison bus and led the caravan of hardcore criminals full steam ahead into the wild lands beyond. They didn't make it fifty yards. Hitting a solid wall of zombies, the bus tires spun uselessly in the muck as the body count piled up. His men blasted shotguns out of the windows while the rest of the convoy arrived on motorcycles and four wheelers. It was gruesome work, but after plenty of gunplay and a little chainsaw action, the bus broke free of the carnage. The Dirty Two-Dozen sped off into the distance.

Heather was unimpressed. "Take me back to my room." Minutes later the two were alone in Marquell's opulent headquarters. He'd taken every nice object in the prison for his own personal space, no matter the interior decorating implications, and the results would have made Saddam Hussein proud. The first lady of the prison put her dog in his tiny bed and sat on the edge of her own. "You have to do whatever I say, right?"

"That's boss's order," Fausto said, wondering what she was after.

She pointed downwards. "Then get to work. I need to relieve some tension."

"I don't think that's what he—"

Heather's temper flared. "You aren't supposed to think, monkey boy."

"Marquell would chop off my *cojones*."

"You saw what happened outside. We won't be seeing them again. Consider this an audition."

Fausto wondered if this was some cruel game to test his loyalty. "He'll be back."

"Don't you want to know how I got Marquell so pussy-whipped?" she said and batted her cold eyes.

"Relax, lady."

"Have you been in prison so long you only like boys? Are you a *chevalla* now?"

"A sissy? Bitch, you must be crazy talking to me like that. Don't you know what I'm capable of?"

Heather was unimpressed. "I know what you've done, but what you're capable of still remains to be seen. Now don't make me tell you again." She hiked up her skirt and revealed smooth skin and a thin black thong.

Fausto rubbed his hands through his hair as the dilemma consumed him. In the end, questioning his machismo proved too much, and the hired gun dropped to his knees in defense of his manhood. Fausto didn't even notice the screwdriver until it penetrated his ear canal and scrambled his brain.

"Typical man," Heather said and pulled the bloody tool out while Fausto writhed on the floor like a beached fish. Finished with the amateur lobotomy, she turned to her puppy that was cowering in the corner. "Mommy won't make you drink the bad stuff again. No more being sick." It turned out that the most conniving person in the prison hadn't been the warden or his replacement.

She calmly went to the window and gave a signal by raising and lowering the blinds. In moments the second prison rebellion began in earnest, and it was even bloodier than the first. Vengeance was swift as the guards clamored for payback, beginning with Sharpshooter Gus opening up on the basketball league with his AR-15 from the safety of the watchtower. From there, the orgy of violence reached every corner of the compound, from the kitchens to the greenhouse to the morgue, with the same results.

The bloodbath was finished in minutes and Marquell's reign was over. If he did make it back, he'd be walking into a buzz saw. For the third time in the prison's short history, there was a new sheriff in town. Only this one had fake boobs, a manicure and a tan.

Chapter 37
Steve Winwood

Charlie brought the women over early on the morning of their planned escape to meet his friends for the first time. It went about as well as expected.

"I wouldn't fuck you if I was on fire and your dick was an extinguisher," Kate replied to a clumsy advance from Left-Nut. He still had it.

"Ah snap," Smokey said while applying war paint to Russ with a permanent marker.

"Oh come on, why not?" Left-Nut asked. "We're all pals here. You wouldn't bend for a friend?"

"Isn't that what you and Mike did?" Russ said, causing the red-faced jerk to shut his mouth.

Charlie waved his hands. "Guys, focus. The sun's rising so there's no room for jacking around." Finally directing the conversation back on topic, they went over the plan one final time and mobilized to make their move.

Trent tied Brandon to his back and prepared to cross the ladder bridge first. "Ready to go, little buddy?" he said, not expecting an answer.

"Elvis," Brandon replied quietly. It was the first time he'd spoken to them.

Shocked, Trent reached back and grabbed the little boy's shoulder. "Elvis is with his family now. In raccoon heaven."

Brandon shook his head and pointed. "No, Elvis."

Sure enough, the rodent with the telltale pirate shirt was sniffing around across the street. Brooke hadn't told Charlie about her dangerous encounter, and everyone still assumed their mascot had been dead.

"I think we should go get him," Trent said and surprised even himself.

Charlie shook his head. "I'm sorry, but no."

Rob disagreed. "You never leave a man behind."

"Raccoon," Charlie corrected.

"You never leave a raccoon behind."

His face covered in ink, Russ stepped forward. "This sounds like a job for someone with my particular skill set. Did I ever tell you how I used to be a bounty hunter?"

Smokey rolled his eyes. "We heard the story. You turned in coyote ears one time, and you ran over the damned thing while getting a b-j from a tranny. Not very hardcore."

"That's not exactly how I remember it."

Charlie sensed a mutiny brewing. "Screw it, I'll drop down and the rest of you get going by roof. I can meet you at the corner. We don't have time for this shit."

"This is dumb," Brooke said, annoyed and nervous at the same time. "Please stick to the plan." Of course, she hadn't told Charlie about the pregnancy yet either and didn't want the father of her child killed while rescuing a raccoon.

"It's settled."

"I'm coming with you then," Smokey said. "I'm scared of heights, and I know what happened to Mike and Jim."

"Fine, we'll give the rest of you a head start and I'll set the music to go off in fifteen minutes." Charlie kissed Brooke deeply and then looked to Rob. "You're in charge. No matter what, make sure Brandon and the girls make it to that helicopter."

Rob nodded. "See you soon."

Ten minutes later, Charlie and Smokey climbed down the blanket ladder after watching the others leapfrog their way to the corner. With the helicopter coming any minute, there was little room for error, and he refused to think about what would happen if it didn't show up.

No zombies were in sight due to their effective culling program, so Charlie and Smokey hustled over and scooped Elvis up, easy like Sunday morning. She was happy to see them and chattered away as they turned to catch the others.

That's when things got interesting. Motorcycles, four-wheelers and finally a bus pulled around the corner and blocked their way, heading right for them. Surrounded by heavily armed men on the smaller vehicles, Charlie and Smokey stood their ground as more filed out of the bus.

A muscle-bound man with a commanding presence came forth while barking out orders. "Doc, get what you need and do it quick." He looked at the captured and now disarmed pair. "You busters have any reason for me to let you live?"

To Charlie's shock, the man before him was the dread-locked prisoner he used to flip off during his daily routine outside the prison. Smokey recognized him too. "Markee, is that you?"

Marquell Washington, pimp, thug and murderer, had also been Smokey's long time dealer, and Smokey had been one hell of a customer. "Ah shit, Smoke, I haven't seen you in a grip. What the fuck's up? I didn't recognize you with that marker all over your face." He slapped hands with his old acquaintance. The two had shared many a blunt over the years, and just like that, the sheer power of stoner luck saved the day. For the moment.

Trent peered through binoculars to assess the situation. "They're surrounded. What do we do now?"

Rob had taken his orders seriously. "Wait and see, but not for long. We'll leave without them if we have to."

Charlie avoided the strongman's gaze as Marquell and Smokey glad-handed. Like usual, Smokey lost track of time and Charlie had to step in. "We need to get going."

"You got something more important to do?" Marquell said as his tone lost its friendliness.

"We're bringing food to some old people. Kinda like meals on wheels."

"Good Samaritans, huh? So where's the food?" Marquell was growing more curious by the second as the doctor emerged with his supplies and the rest of his men beat to death several zombies lured by the sound of running engines. The crooks appeared to be enjoying it.

"We gotta find it first," Charlie replied unconvincingly.

In prison, one is completely surrounded by liars, and Marquell had naturally learned to recognize most tells — to him, Charlie's arched eyebrow was screaming bullshit. "Carrying a pet would only slow you down," he said as his men closed in. "You hiding something from me, bro?"

"Maybe they got some bitches nearby," one of Marquell's lackeys said. The breaking and entering expert with a unibrow and bad haircut got right into Charlie's face.

"Yeah, or drugs," another said after using a lead pipe to deliver a deathblow to a downed zombie.

Defying their very nature, Trent and Russ left the group behind and snuck towards their captured friends, moving from one hiding spot to another. With only a pistol and shovel, it wasn't quite clear what they hoped to accomplish, but Trent stepping up was no small miracle in itself.

Marquell now looked Charlie square in the eye. "Your bald ass looks familiar."

Charlie silently cursed himself for derailing the plan and hoped the others were sticking to it. "I get that a lot, my mom said it's because—"

"Yeah, I'm sure of it." Marquell's voice rose. "You're the motherfucker that used to talk shit to me every day."

It was at that exact second the stereo kicked on, playing Steve Winwood's "Back in the High Life Again," cranked up so loud anyone within a mile could hear it. The thugs looked around in bewilderment as the dinner bell rang, and zombies poured in from all directions, jumping through windows, running out of buildings and even rising out of an open manhole.

Marquell quickly forgot about Charlie as deadly hand to mouth combat began. The prisoners shot, stabbed, and bludgeoned their attackers by the dozens, but were quickly overwhelmed by the growing army of the dead. It was simple math.

The prisoner with the unibrow panicked and fled on a four-wheeler when one of his friends rose from the ground, freshly zombie-fied. Never one for cowardice, the boss shot him down in cold blood. "Kill anyone that runs!"

Charlie grabbed the dead man's gun and dove behind a car with Smokey as Trent and Russ made their way over, now contending with incoming zombies and stray bullets. At this point, Elvis, the reason they were even in this predicament, ran off in the commotion.

That's when the bus blew up and sent flaming debris and shrapnel amidst the combatants. Sergeant Zhang's forces had been drawn by Steve Winwood's smooth voice and the roar of battle, and they unleashed a volley of type 69 RPG's to announce their arrival. They sprayed the area with automatic fire and things really got ugly.

"Fuck this." Russ threw his shovel and ducked down an alleyway before disappearing behind the buildings.

"Goddammit, Russ!" Trent screamed while firing at zombies, prisoners and Chinamen alike. He soon reached his pinned down friends and narrowly avoided a hail of bullets that flew past him and tore into a nearby zombie instead. "Fatality," he said after firing a round into the face of the twitching creature on the ground. It had been Marquell's conscripted doctor minutes earlier.

"I never thought I'd be glad to see you," Charlie said and fired at a soldier trying to flank them, finally hitting the man on his third shot. "Where's everyone else?"

"They're headed to the pickup zone. Except for Russ. He bailed and—" Trent was interrupted by the sound of a low-flying helicopter. It raked the People's Liberation Army with rounds and took off, chased by a withering assault of small arms fire and RPG's .

Seeing the enemy distracted, Marquell crawled out from under several corpses and slid across the hood of the car, crashing into Smokey. "Don't shoot man, same team," he said quickly as Trent raised his pistol.

Charlie nodded. "He's right, it's gonna take all of us to get out of here. What we gotta do is—"

Heavy machine gun fire rained down on the Chinese position from overhead, interrupting Charlie's plan but giving them an opening just the same. Shouts of, "Get some, get some, get some!" rang out, meaning Russ was deep in the midst of an imaginary Vietnam War flashback. He might have been a deadbeat dad, a petty thief and a statutory rapist, but he was also a patriotic son of a bitch.

Instead of fleeing, Russ had made his way to the back of the apartment and scaled the alley gate in order to reach Trent's window. From there it was a quick trip upstairs to unleash his fury on the invading army. Having the high ground and a clear shot, he was knocking them down like bowling pins.

By this point, most of the prisoners had fallen to bullets or bites, and the "good guys" were seriously outnumbered. Still, Russ kept up his onslaught and dozens of freshly made zombies added to the mayhem.

But the soldiers kept coming too, and it didn't take long for Russ to run out of ammo. Like a man possessed, he jumped off the back of the building and twisted in midair, his mullet flowing in the wind as he grabbed the chain link fence on his way down. It was glorious, until Zombie Cliff sprang at the fence and bit Russ's finger off in one jerky motion. The toothless and dehydrated nightmare's rictus grin revealed a jagged jaw sharpened by months of gnawing on brick walls.

"Son of a bitch." Russ flipped Cliff off with his remaining middle finger. His next move was to bash in the window of Smokey's hybrid SUV and grab the keys under the seat. If there was anything deadlier than a drunken suicidal redneck with a machine gun, it was a drunken suicidal redneck behind the wheel. As Steve Winwood continued on repeat above the din of battle, Russ blasted through one gate and then the other, obliterating Cliff and bursting onto the main street, seventy starving zombies in tow.

Bullets riddled the car and the zombies on top of it, yet Russ drove right into the ranks of the invading troops, acting as a blocker for the bloodthirsty crowd behind him. It was a massacre and General Zhang was the first to be swept away by the hungry zombie tidal wave.

Charlie, Smokey and even Marquell cheered as the momentum shifted and the Chinese soldiers broke ranks and fled with the cannibals in hot pursuit. That's when Charlie noticed Trent was gone. Apparently, the cop's heroism had limits and after cheating death one too many times, his scumbag side came roaring back with a vengeance. He'd used Russ's distraction to slip away unnoticed.

Meanwhile, Russ was about to pull around for a victory lap when he realized his steering and brakes were out. And the engine was on fire. And the local swimming pool was right in front of him. He lit a cigarette with his good hand and went through one more fence before crashing into the deep end.

The SUV began to sink as dirty water rushed in and Russ's stomach began to churn. He took a drag from the cigarette while engine smoke filled the car and a handful of zombies splashed into the water above him. "And they said THESE would kill me."

Chapter 38
Fancy Meeting You Here

Rob fought back the urge to rescue his friends when the music started and the shit hit the fan. But this was the first time he'd ever been in charge of something important, and he was not going to fail. He'd had a lifetime of that already. Big Rob Magnusson the idiot, the dirty kid, the punching bag, the laughingstock. Not today.

They watched in horror as the zombies swarmed by and then in shock as the Chinese troops arrived. Still, Rob maintained a steady demeanor and kept them focused by repeating the plan like a mantra. "Go down the ladder, two blocks north, one block west, everyone follow me. Go down the ladder, two blocks north, one block west, everyone follow me."

The flow of cannibals past their position slowed to a trickle, and when the helicopter flew by, it was game time. Rob zoomed down the ladder and effortlessly split a slow moving zombie's skull in half with the whirl of his bat. Left-Nut followed with Brandon while the women huddled in close behind. There was no turning back.

Charlie's plan had crumbled through a volatile mixture of stupidity, bad luck, and bravery. Now they were crossing no man's land in early daylight during the middle of a battle royal. A casual observer probably would've expected their escape to turn out exactly like this.

The refugees made quick progress and only slowed down long enough for Rob to annihilate whatever hapless zombie was dumb enough to give chase. He was performing like a gladiator and it didn't matter if the zombies came two or three at a time. Headshot, broken spine, broken neck, splattered face, over and over. He had help too, with Brooke firing away until her pistol was empty while Kate put a cast-iron skillet to good use. Left-Nut continued to carry Brandon and simply positioned himself between the others as blockers. His self-preservation skills were finally put to good use.

Covered in blood and entrails, the genial giant now looked like he was straight out of a b-horror movie. At one point, the killing tool slipped from Rob's hand and forced him to assume his old wrestling stance. He maneuvered around one assailant and power bombed it onto the sidewalk like a ripe pumpkin.

Kate wiped the bat clean on her shirt and handed it back. "Almost there," she said with a mixture of disgust and encouragement on her face.

They went around the corner and found the helicopter parked ahead as promised. Fifty yards to go. Forty. Thirty. The Black Hawk fired on several nearby zombies and the group waved frantically to avoid getting shot as well. Twenty yards, so close that the downwash battered their clothes and blew the women's hair around.

One last zombie approached and Rob unleashed every remaining bit of rage he had left. The aluminum bat bent on impact and the broken beast tumbled end over end before stopping in a pile of shattered death. Success.

Before Rob knew what was happening, Kate grabbed him by the jaw and planted a passionate kiss on his lips. Left-Nut lined up for his own smooch and was quickly turned down. He still had it.

The soldiers gave a warm greeting, checked them for bites, and brought Brandon into the cockpit. Next, they strapped the women in while a still blushing Rob grabbed the gunner's shoulder. "Can you wait five minutes?"

As though on cue, more zombies streamed towards the helicopter, and the gunner effortlessly mowed them down. "We're leaving now," the man said unemotionally. "This city's a goddamned graveyard and we're not coming back."

Rob stepped out of the helicopter. "Where are you going to take them?"

"There's a camp due south of Cantonville. Do you know the area?" the man asked.

Big Rob beamed a toothy smile. "Know it? That's where we grew up." He reached in and forcefully dragged Left-Nut off the helicopter.

"What the fuck are you doing?"

"Never leave a man behind, remember?"

Brooke made eye contact with Rob as the chopper took off. "Tell Charlie I'm pregnant!"

Viking Rob Magnusson picked up his bent baseball bat, grabbed his cursing friend by the scruff of the neck, and headed towards the sound of gunfire.

*   *   *

Trent was jolted awake by what he hoped was a bucket of warm water splashing into his face. Helpless and scared, he strained against his bonds in the darkness, only making them slick with blood.

The dirty cop had abandoned his friends an hour earlier and against his own intuition, snuck inside the Halloween store. It was his nature to be a coward after all, and as things headed seriously south, it was the obvious choice. But he hadn't even shut the door when a hard object crashed upside his head and knocked him out cold. Now he was at the tender mercy of whatever lurked in the pitch darkness. He could hear it moving closer.

"Uh hello," Trent said and played his best average Joe routine. "I'm a cop." His jaw hurt like hell and was most likely dislocated. Possibly broken.

His captor turned on a flashlight and revealed a slender person wearing a translucent clown mask with makeup haphazardly smeared across the face. Trent hated clowns. The thing crept forward as liquid hit the floor.

"A fear piss? God you're such a pussy," came the familiar female voice. It was absolutely the last one he expected to hear. Sarah Birdsong removed the mask and was even prettier than he remembered. On the downside, she had turned pants-crapping insane.

"Thank God you survi—"

A fist flew out of the darkness and solidly connected with Trent's eye socket, rocking his head against the metal chair. "You rancid piece of shit," Sarah said with bile rising in her throat.

"I'm sorry I—"

Another punch cut him off. "Shut it."

"Sarah, I'm different now. I was scared."

She covered his mouth with duct tape. "You're not talking your way out of this. I do suppose you're wondering what's going on. After you abandoned me, I shot so many bastards crawling into the car it was like a cocoon of dead bodies. And I was there for a whole day until somebody cut me out. Do you know how much pain I was in?" She patted his head. "You will."

Sarah pulled up a chair. "After an elderly couple nursed me back to health, I made my way over here. Of course, like the herpes you gave me and lied about, you were still around."

Trent continued to quietly work at the tape around his wrists, but the more he strained, the farther it pushed into his flesh.

"Then I watched and waited and hoped you'd screw up. By the way, you and your idiot friends snuck up on me a while back. One of those mannequins was me. I just stood still and you morons walked right by me."

The tape began to tear. A little more and he'd have an arm free. She continued, unaware and clearly enjoying her captive audience's discomfort. "You called me a badge bunny, a holster sniffer. You even sexted my naked pictures around the department. And you know, I could forgive all that. But what kind of human shit-stain leaves an injured person behind like you did?"

She finally noticed Trent's efforts to escape and laughed heartily. "You're not getting off that easy." Sarah re-taped his limbs to the chair and made sure to rip the long hair off his arms in the process. "And I watched your friends leave, so don't expect any last minute James Bond-type rescues. No, you're going to hear what I have to say for once in your life. Then you're going to feel the same pain that I did. And then you're going to die."

Chapter 39
Road Trippin'

"**W**hy didn't she tell me she was pregnant?" Charlie said upon hearing the news.

Left-Nut smirked. "Who says it's yours?" At least he'd finally stopped cursing at Rob.

Oddly enough, this revelation hit Charlie harder than the recent death and destruction had. "Of all the times to be a dad. And what if I never find them?"

"Maybe you shouldn't have left her for that rat?" Left-Nut said, and the look he received in return could have melted his face off.

"It's really touching," Marquell said as he loaded several Chinese assault rifles onto the back of an ATV. "But this ain't the place to be sharing y'alls motherfuckin' feelings right now."

Rob noticed they were missing members from their group. "Where's Russ?"

Charlie looked down. "Russ's gone. He sure went out in a blaze of glory, though."

"And Trent?"

Charlie's expression turned from sorrow to anger. "Piece of shit ran off. I knew he'd wind up screwing us."

"Kinda like the way a monkey always ends up fucking a football," Smokey said. "You know it's going to, but it still surprises you when it happens."

Rob sighed deeply. "He was doing so good there for a while, especially with Brandon."

"What's plan B?" Left-Nut asked. "I mean, your first one worked out so great."

"We could fight our way through downtown. Now we got grenades and stuff," Rob said and shrugged.

Charlie pointed to the mounds of dead soldiers. "That didn't help them much."

"Okay, what then?" Left-Nut said.

Charlie had already weighed the pros and cons of several routes and settled on one in particular. "Main roads and highways aren't an option. There's too many zombies and who knows how many Chinese assholes out there, so we'll head south to the Blue Line tracks and take them west to the Metra Tracks. Then we follow the forest preserves and power lines all the way home."

"Seems like a lot of dicking around," Left-Nut said. "Why not hit the highways and haul ass? I could be banging your sister by lunchtime."

"This way we avoid blocked roads and checkpoints. It's about ninety miles to my parents' place once we get outside the city. That base Rob talked about is just south of there."

Marquell seriously pondered the idea of shooting his new acquaintances just to get them to shut up, but he knew there was no point. Plus, they had saved his life, and loyalty was the one virtue the killer respected. "Good luck with that shit," he said and hopped on a four-wheeler. "I got my dog's medicine and food, so I'm out."

"They all died for your dog?" Charlie said, dumbfounded.

"Didn't you just risk lives for a damned raccoon?" came the reply. Charlie nodded and Marquell continued. "If ya'll ever want work and don't mind getting your hands dirty, come see me. Later Smokey." With that, The Butcher of Richard Daley Prison left.

The guys would never know how lucky they were to survive their encounter with Marquell, but they were far from being in the clear. For starters, many of those recently dispatched were stirring from their temporary deaths. Rob used his crooked bat to clobber a nearby zombie as it struggled to rise on shattered legs. "We need to decide."

"It's my way or the highway, literally," Charlie said and climbed onto one of the remaining four-wheelers. Smokey jumped behind him and Rob and Left-Nut took the other. His way it was.

Moments later, the survivors sped south full throttle into their next half-baked scheme. They hadn't seen any foreign invaders, but zombies were a different story. Soon a veritable apocalyptic army swarmed behind them and was growing by the block. One wrong turn and it was curtains.

"How much gas do we have?" Smokey asked while hanging on for dear life as the wind blew his long brown hair straight back.

Charlie looked at the gauge for the first time. "Enough to get to the burbs."

"We're running out of gas," Rob said as he pulled up next to them.

"Oh come on." Charlie stopped next to an overpass as the crowd drew nearer, three hundred yards and closing. "Go ahead and find a garden hose in someone's yard and start siphoning. We'll slow these jagoffs down and meet you at the tracks."

Rob nodded and peeled out as Charlie and Smokey steadied their machine guns across the seat. "Fuck, how do you shoot this thing?" Smokey said while searching for the safety. Charlie had the same problem as the crowd neared.

TATATATATATATATATATAT!

Smokey's gun discharged and sent bullets through the windows of nearby buildings. "Here it is." He fired in earnest and began dropping zombies by the handful. "It's a turkey shoot!" he added as shell casings sprinkled around them. Unfortunately, many were merely wounded and rejoined the others in their deadly march.

Charlie also blasted away but the enemy kept coming like waves at the beach. Both guns clicked empty. "Um, how do we reload?" Smokey asked.

Charlie shrugged his shoulders. "Cheese it," he said and jumped onto the four-wheeler.

Smokey turned to follow but was stopped as bodies crashed all around him, falling from the overpass and hitting the pavement with sickening, wet thuds. Heavy breathing and the sound of gnashing teeth came next as the crawling monsters clamored for sustenance, grasping at the stoner's exposed legs.

Charlie calmly drew his pistol and ended the three ghouls with well-placed headshots. Smokey climbed aboard as Charlie retrieved a fragmentation grenade, pulled the pin, and tossed it towards the surging multitude.

BOOOM! Body parts and shrapnel zipped by while they took off, barely fast enough to avoid the survivors. But avoid them they did, and the maniacs were quickly left behind with nothing to show for their efforts but gaping wounds and internal bleeding. Charlie was on top of his game once again.

The tracks loomed up ahead and gunfire signaled that the area wasn't as empty as Charlie had hoped. Rob and Left-Nut were busy fending off their own crowd of savages.

Charlie pulled up long enough to watch how Rob reloaded and then took off again with his friends close behind. Soon they zoomed down the tracks, avoiding abandoned trains, dead bodies, and of course, zombies, zombies and more zombies.

Every tunnel brought more challenges now that they had to rely solely on headlights and muzzle flashes to lead the way. Because of this, their trips underground became a blur of shooting and screaming, near misses and carnage. Each subterranean nightmare lasted only a few minutes, and everyone breathed a huge sigh of relief upon bursting into the light for the final time, figuratively reborn. Except for Left-Nut.

"Wow, check out your hair," Smokey said as they got into the open.

Left-Nut frantically touched his head. "What, what is it?" Miraculously, his already pale locks had turned a few shades whiter from the insanity of the tunnels.

"Your head's whiter than Gandalf's balls," Smokey said with a laugh and received a middle finger in return.

Left-Nut's condition was of no concern other than comic relief, and the trip down the Metra railway continued, growing easier as they reached further into the suburbs. Now they went miles at a time without spotting a zombie, and the few stragglers they did see were easily avoided.

They followed the tracks into a thickly wooded preserve where the cover of the forest allowed them to regroup in the shade of some tall oak trees. A swiftly flowing river nearby gave off a calming aura, and the men stretched out while breathing in the fresh air. It had been the longest morning of their lives.

"That's the Des Plaines River," Charlie said and checked his tires for leaks. "Which means Maywood is right on the other side of the bridge. We can cross over and follow the power lines that go by two-ninety. Those will run all the way to Cantonville."

"You pulling this straight out of your butt?" Rob asked and drank from a thermos attached to his vehicle. Charlie nodded and Rob slapped him on the shoulder, a little too hard. "Keep it up, muchacho."

After relaxing and making fun of Left-Nut for several minutes, the journey began again amidst rising spirits. As they crossed a narrow stone bridge, Charlie finally believed they could survive the trip. Then something whizzed past his head and bounced across the water below like a rock skipped by a child.

The crack of the rifle caught up a second later, and more splashes hit the water followed by bullets ricocheting off the tracks. A Chinese checkpoint on another bridge had spotted them and opened fire. Only a hundred and fifty yards separated them.

"Punch it!" Charlie yelled and slammed on the gas as a hail of bullets peppered the ground all around them. They sped off the bridge and lurched down an embankment with Rob's ATV nearly tipping over in the process. He used his massive frame to muscle two tires back to the ground and kept right on going while Left-Nut clung to him like a terrified girlfriend.

Having solved the mystery of the missing zombies, the guys now had to avoid running into another patrol. So they cruised through the charred ruins of Maywood at top speed. Soon the massive transmission towers loomed dead ahead. In normal life, the hundred and eighty-foot tall structures had been easy to ignore, but seeing the steel behemoths up close for the first time was simply awe-inspiring. More importantly, the open ground below them went on as far as the eye could see. They entered the path and never looked back, leaving the hell of the dead city behind for good.

The group stopped an hour later to let their engines cool down. Having prepared ahead, Charlie cracked open a fanny pack full of teriyaki beef jerky.

"Nice fanny pack, homo," Left-Nut said, though he didn't put much effort into it.

"You don't want any?" Charlie asked, not bothering to point out that Left-Nut actually had engaged in gay sex.

Of course he wanted some, and Charlie divvied up the dehydrated meat as evenly as possible. It was the last of their food and everyone savored each bite of the salty treat.

"It's time for a celebration bitches," Smokey said while pulling out a thick joint from his pocket. "Marquell hooked me up for old-time's sake."

"I'll pass," Charlie said. "But go ahead and blaze up. You earned it."

The others partook and within minutes were coughing and blowing smoke rings into the wind like bored high schoolers. Time slowed and their stress levels dropped. It seemed Marquell still had good shit.

They finished smoking and saddled up for the last leg of their fantastic journey, a fifty-mile straight shot through the countryside. Five minutes later, however, right as they had achieved maximum buzz, several figures appeared in the distance. Zombies, five burly construction workers to be precise, milled about the base of a transmission tower.

"Go around," Charlie said. "No need to waste ammo." As they got closer, though, it appeared there was more to the story. Two men were perched thirty feet up the structure, and they were shouting for help.

The zombies turned and gave chase when they heard the four-wheelers approach, scrambling past each other in their bloodlust. Charlie and Rob pulled over and dropped them in an instant with a volley of bullets. It had become trivial.

Smokey noticed something peculiar as the strangers climbed down. One zombie, a half-naked woman, had been motionless before they got there. He verified she was dead as Left-Nut peeked over his shoulder. "Not bad," the pervert said with a leer. "Is she still warm?"

The two sweaty men, state troopers as evidenced by their clothing, finally reached the ground. They looked like they hadn't slept in days and smelled even worse. "Thanks. I don't know how much longer we could have held on," the taller of them said. "Do you have anything to drink? I was about to drink my own piss."

Rob handed over his thermos and the man chugged with gusto, spilling much of it down his shirt. Then his throat exploded like a burst water balloon.

Without warning, Smokey had raised his machine gun and killed the man instantly. He turned to shoot the other trooper but the guy sprang upon him and wrestled for control of the weapon, spraying bullets in every direction.

Rob's brawny hands wrapped around the man's neck from behind, and after a quick twist and a loud pop, it was all over but the twitching. The trooper's body slumped to the ground next to his lifeless partner. Smokey's heavy breathing was the only sound as he rose and tried to compose himself.

"Well, that escalated quickly, "Left-Nut said and popped out from behind one of the four-wheelers.

"What the shit?" Charlie said, his mouth gaping open at the actions of his mild-mannered friends. "I mean, what kind of weed was that?"

"I was just following Smokey," Rob said and looked at his hands in horror.

"It wasn't the weed." Smokey calmly approached the girl's corpse and pointed to underwear wrapped around the dead teenager's neck. "I've seen a lot of dead zombies, but I never saw one strangled with lacy panties before. Plus she has no visible bites and that's a classic ligature mark."

Charlie wasn't convinced by Smokey's deductive process. "Dude, you just murdered those guys."

"And check out the uniforms. They don't fit, and look at the short one's nametag." Smokey pointed to the man with the broken neck. "Have you ever seen a guy with curly red hair named Ramirez?"

"So?" Charlie said.

"These guys weren't law enforcement any more than you're a cowboy or Rob's a Viking. They obviously stole the uniforms, raped and strangled that poor girl, maybe not even in that order, and then climbed the tower when these dickweeds surprised them."

"You killed them on a hunch?" Charlie pressed.

"Wake up. They were gonna waste us and take our shit the first chance they got, guaranteed. Probably would have raped Left-Nut too while they were at it."

"Okay, Sherlock, explain to me how you know all this."

"Do you have any idea how many episodes of *Special Victims Unit* I've watched? Like, probably all of them. This is second nature to me."

"That Mariska Hargitay is a total smokeshow for an older chick," Left-Nut added. "I use to jerky my turkey to her all the time."

"A little respect, guys?" Charlie closed the dead girl's eyes and then covered her up with a reflective vest from one of the dispatched zombies.

Left-Nut's face turned red in anger as he pointed to the ATVs. "Beautiful." One leaked gas and the other poured out green radiator fluid. Both were ruined. "And I swear I heard banjoes playing earlier."

The grim reality that their trip would continue by foot settled in, and nobody talked as they somberly dragged the corpses into a pile. After stacking leaves and tinder for kindling, Charlie said a few words and then put to flame the bodies of the poor girl and hapless zombies. Coyotes and crows would take care of the rapists.

"What do we do now?" Rob asked while the crackling funeral pyre became fully engulfed in flame, bathing them with an intense heat.

"We go home," Charlie said wistfully, almost to himself. Here was that change of scenery he'd wanted. They silently unloaded their gear and headed for the tree line, each lost in his own thoughts.

It was a beautiful day for a walk in the countryside, with the leaves changing and the temperature hitting that magical seventies sweet spot. The sickly-sweet scent of burning bodies followed them across the fields for quite a while, finally replaced by the smells of fall, and maybe a little rain in the distance.

Epilogue

Sarah Birdsong beat her partner until he passed out. Then she woke him up to do it again. And again. Unluckily for Trent, she was getting bored and there was only one thing left to do. She grabbed the paring knife already used to slice the skin off his knuckles and approached the bound man with a wry smile. "This is it, buddy boy."

Trent prayed to God for the first time in his life. He didn't expect an answer.

KSSSSHHHH! The storefront window shattered as a body crashed through it, blinding the two cops with light from outside. Sarah turned to run but Trent used every muscle of his body to kick through the tape holding him back, and he tripped her up with one final act of revenge.

The zombie pounced on her and instantly began to feast. Trent couldn't see what was happening at his feet but the guttural screaming and kicking told the story in grim detail. The melee stopped and Sarah was obviously dead, which meant Trent was now set to be dessert. He was out of the frying pan and into the fire, so to speak.

The creature stood up, naked and grinning with blood dripping from its mouth like barbecue sauce. Trent instantly recognized the long flowing mullet with a signature bald patch. The zombie was Blake's Uncle Russ.

Russ nonchalantly pulled the knife sticking out of his arm and then raised his hands up like a caricature of Frankenstein. Mere inches from Trent's face, Russ opened his bloody mouth wide and... laughed.

"I got you good, man. Did you piss your pants?"

Of course, Trent couldn't answer with his mouth taped shut. This was a particular problem because Sarah was slowing standing up and an oblivious Russ kept right on blabbering away. The cop tried blinking rapidly to get his attention. It didn't work.

"Fucking Cliff bit me and I ended up crashing Smokey's car. FYI, you get a major case of firehole when you become a zombie. Shit myself something awful, so I came here for some new duds. Then I heard the chick going on and on about killing you. It also turns out zombies have great hearing. Who knew?"

Freshly zombified herself, Sarah came to her senses and dove past Russ, landing on top of Trent and knocking the chair backwards with a crash. That was as far as she got. Russ buried the knife to its hilt in Sarah's heart and then pushed her limp body to the side. She was dead for good this time.

He continued talking as if nothing had happened. "So I figured I could find something to wear in here. Maybe like a Johnny Depp pirate outfit or something. I already got the hair." He ripped the tape from Trent's mouth.

"Ouch. Wait, so are you a zombie or not? What the fuck's going on?"

"I think so," he said while licking his lips. "That bitch did taste like steak." Russ didn't know it, but he'd hit the genetic jackpot. Years of huffing paint combined with massive amounts of nitrates from a beef jerky and cat food diet had altered key brain cells drastically. The result was a partial immunity to the killer virus, making him the world's only zombie-human hybrid. Russ had been dead drunk for years. Now it was official.

"Cut me loose. And put some clothes on, shit."

Russ nodded and pointed to Sarah. "Yeah, I better. That hot little number's giving me bit of a zom-boner if you know what I mean."

Russ freed his friend and then found the pirate outfit he'd been looking for. While he changed, a bruised and battered Trent wrapped up his own bloodied hands and pondered the recent events. There was no reason he should have lived, and yet, here he was. The veteran cop believed strange coincidences simply didn't happen in life, and that he must have survived for a reason.

He thought of that reason as they walked outside. "You know Russ, it's possible your dumb ass might be the savior of the world."

"I'm listening."

"Maybe scientists can make a cure from your blood or something. Like in the movies." Russ shrugged and Trent continued. "I'm gonna make sure we find out."

They picked around the wreckage for anything useful and settled on two motorcycles in decent condition. While searching for the keys, Trent found a note stuck to the tire of a smoldering ATV. He read it aloud.

Dear Dickhead (Trent),

If you are reading this, it means you're still alive. We're going to Charlie's mom and dad's house, and hope to meet up with Brandon and the girls soon after. There is supposed to be a military base nearby. Come find us if you can. Or whatever,

Smokey

Spoiler Alert, Charlie's pissed at you.

Trent laughed. "I really think the Lord's telling me something." Russ rolled his vacant, creepy eyes and Trent crumpled the paper and tossed it towards the gutter. It bounced off a raccoon.

"Come here, you little bugger," Russ said. Elvis happily scampered up his back before settling on the zombie's shoulder. He adjusted Little E's tiny pirate costume. "Look at that, we match. I don't have to get a parrot after all."

Even though he was in extreme pain, Trent hadn't felt this good in a long time. He now had a purpose. "We need a name for our group."

Russ climbed onto his jet-black Harley and turned the engine on. The steel machine rumbled with power while he took a swig from a flask of whiskey and replaced the cap. "That's easy. Bad Company." Elvis chirped in approval.

"I like it," Trent said and started his own motorcycle, a purple chopper with a naked woman painted on the side. But then something strange happened, as if strangeness even registered anymore with these guys. Like out of a dream, a group of giraffes came around the corner and wandered right towards them.

"That beautiful gay bastard pulled it off," Trent said without a trace of malice. "Way to go, Mike!"

The odds of a born again cop, a raccoon, a drunk zombie and several giraffes meeting peacefully at the corner of Armitage and Damon were a trillion to one, but that's exactly what happened. The gentle creatures nibbled on a few leaves and then moved on in search of greener pastures elsewhere. Like all survivors, they were going to have a long winter.

Trent took a deep breath. "Let's go save the world," he said. "And one more thing, you're not gonna eat me, right?"

Russ pulled away as Elvis peeked over the handlebars. "No promises."

Acknowledgments

I would like to thank all of the people who have helped me finish this project as well as those who have given me tons of encouragement along the way.

Big thanks go out to Derek Murphy of Creativindie Covers for creating such an eye-catching cover design, and to the crew at ManuscriptMagic.com for their excellent copyediting work.

Thank you to my friends and family for believing in me, thank you to my lovely wife Kristin and my boys Kevin and Ryan for being there for me, and thank you to my parents for allowing me to watch gory zombie movies at an inappropriately young age.

Most importantly, thank you for taking interest in my book.

About the Author

Richard Johnson is a writer and small business owner who grew up in Galesburg, Illinois during the 80's. He graduated from Monmouth College as a double major in History and English and earned a Masters degree in History with a teaching certificate from Western Illinois University. He currently lives with his growing family in a small town outside of Chicago.

Richard is a self-acclaimed expert in the zombie genre after spending countless hours watching B-rated horror movies. He is a good friend, a bad cook and a terrible dancer. If a real zombie apocalypse strikes, seek him out for protection. But bring plenty of beer.